Spit in the Ocean

Jake Samson Mysteries by Shelley Singer:

SAMSON'S DEAL
FREE DRAW
FULL HOUSE
SPIT IN THE OCEAN

SPIT IN THE OCEAN

A Jake Samson Mystery

SHELLEY SINGER

*Pat — hope you like
this one — Gds !
Shelley S*

St. Martin's Press · New York

Design by John Fontana

Library of Congress Cataloging-in-Publication Data

Singer, Shelley.
  Spit in the ocean.

  I. Title.
PS3569.I565S6 1987   813'.54   87-4408
ISBN 0-312-00685-3

First Edition

10 9 8 7 6 5 4 3 2 1

for Elizabeth Lay

My thanks to Barbara Raboy, for sharing her expertise, and to Paula, for the use of her files.

—1—

Nothing is colder, windier, wetter, and more miserable than the northern California coast in January.

Nothing is more beautiful.

So it was with mixed emotions, heavy boots, and a long yellow slicker that I drove splashing down the main street of Wheeler just a few days after New Year's, headed for the Oceanview Motel.

A motel, yes, but the trip had nothing to do with a love affair—at least not mine. It had everything to do with the sex lives of hundreds of people I had never met.

I had seen the story in the *San Francisco Chronicle* just a couple of days before I got the phone call from my pal Chloe Giannapoulos. It seemed that a friend of hers was the founder of a company called the North Coast Sperm Bank, which had been the victim of an act of vandalism. Someone had broken into their storage area, stolen all their frozen stock, and left a note saying they were "setting it free" in the ocean. There was no reason not to believe the note, since the local law had found the containers littering the water along the beach.

Apparently, though, Chloe's friend was not satisfied with what the police had done, or not done, since then. She felt, Chloe said, that they just weren't taking the crime seriously enough.

Chloe told her friend that she knew a guy who would, for a fee, take the crime very seriously and probably even solve it. So there I was.

I parked my car in the side lot of the Oceanview, near the office, pulled my suitcase and yellow slicker out of the backseat, and made my way through a rising wind up slick wooden steps to a door so swollen with wetness it took a well-placed foot to get it open.

The man at the desk smiled a "welcome traveler" smile which broadened into a "welcome tourist" smile when he realized I was going to be staying for a while. I figured he didn't see many tourists this time of year. During the rainy season not many outlanders stop by for a bite of seafood and long walks on the beach. No tourists from the Midwest, and damned few from Oakland.

"Hope you enjoy your visit," he said. "Looks like you're in for some bad weather."

I assured him that I would have a good time anyway.

"Anyplace good to pick up a fast lunch around here?" I asked. I hadn't eaten before leaving home, and I had an hour before my three o'clock appointment with Chloe's friend. I'd noticed a café just down the street, but I wanted a local recommendation. He said Georgia's Café—the one I'd spotted—was very good.

My room looked out on the parking lot. I tossed my stuff on the bed and went to the window. There were a couple of big, brittle eucalyptus trees at the edge of the lot, not fifty feet from my car. Eucalyptus tends to leave pieces of itself lying around in good weather, and in bad it can lose very large pieces. I could only pray that these would aim no limbs at my 1953 blue and white Chevy Bel Air.

I left it sitting there and walked the block and a half to Georgia's through a steady rain. Just inside the door were a couple of bentwood hatracks hung with dripping rainwear. I added mine and took a two-person booth.

Half a dozen people were scattered around a room that could hold maybe three dozen. The bits of conversation I could hear were all about the weather.

The waitress brought me a menu, said hello pleasantly, and, as though she were continuing an earlier conversation, told me it looked like we were in for a gale. I ordered a hamburger with everything, for sustenance. She went away again and I tuned in on a nearby group of three men, drinking coffee and eating doughnuts.

". . . never washed away yet," a large, white-faced man was saying.

One of his friends laughed. "There's always a first time, Henry. I've seen waves hit that spit hard enough and high enough to wash right across the road. I never could understand why you picked that spot to build on."

Henry shrugged. "The houses are on high ground. And I like it out there. It's pretty."

His friend laughed again. "You just like the company." He turned to the third man. "He likes living around the rich and famous, like you do." The third man shook his gray head and took another bite of his doughnut, another sip of his coffee. His fingernails were black. "I just hope none of those rich and famous houses wash away tonight."

"Doesn't matter," the third man grunted, wiping his mouth with his dirty hand. "They don't live there anyway. Besides, might be God's judgment."

"Oh, come on, Frank, you don't believe that," Henry said.

The second man, the youngest of the three, shook his head and spoke—petulantly, I thought. "Problem is, while they're flying around in jet planes, I'm the guy who has to keep an eye on their investments." He stood up and turned to go, and that was when I noticed that his khaki shirt was part of a uniform and that a badge was pinned to it. He said good-bye to his friends.

They finished their coffee in silence. I finished my meal,

had a second cup of coffee, and decided, despite the weather, to walk to my appointment. According to the directions I'd gotten over the phone the day before, my destination was a good half mile away, near the other end of the business section. But I'd be walking away from the ocean, with the wind at my back, and after a better-than-two-hour drive from Oakland in the first place, I wanted the exercise.

—2—

The sperm bank was located, appropriately enough, in a building that had once served another kind of bank, a now-defunct financial institution whose name, carved into the stone above the door, remained. All very solid, right down to the phony columns on either side of the glass door, which was now lettered with the words, "North Coast Cryobank." The rest of the block looked less than prosperous: to the left, a vacant lot; to the right, a tired-looking dress shop.

The bank's first floor had been cut up and walled so the visitor saw nothing on entering but a reception desk, a five-foot schefflera in a plastic planter, and a few chairs. When I walked in, the woman behind the desk smiled warmly, glanced to her left to make sure the lounging private guard hadn't gone to the toilet or anything, and asked what she could do for me. I told her. She pushed some buttons, got an okay to send me along, and directed me to an exit door to my right. "Just go up the stairs, third office on the left."

I knocked on the partly open door, right below the little plastic placard that said "Nora Canfield," no title, and was told to "come right in."

Canfield, I knew, was the executive director. I expected to see some kind of secretarial desk right inside, but instead walked directly into the executive office. I didn't know how to feel about that. Was I supposed to be impressed by the lack of pretension? Was all this informality really unselfconscious?

She stood and extended her hand across the desk. "Nora Canfield," she said. "I'm glad you could come, Mr. Samson."

We got past all the "no, just call me Jake" stuff and I sat down, on a comfortable, California-style first-name basis with the boss of what looked to be a pretty good-sized business.

Despite the casual office setup, this was not a particularly casual woman. She was dressed in neat slacks with a sharp crease and a tailored blouse of some silky material. She had soft-looking dark brown hair, cut short, brown eyes, and a full mouth. She did not smile, and the brown eyes and full mouth were all business. So was her office, which was painted in muted, tranquil colors and contained little in the way of ornament. She had one window, which looked out over the backyard of some kind of shop that fronted the main street.

She got right to it.

"Chloe tells me you've had a lot of experience in this sort of thing."

"Not exactly," I said. "Murders and disappearances, that's what I've handled so far. I don't know anything about your business, and I've never dealt with burglary. And you should know I have no license to operate as a private detective."

She waved a hand at me. "I don't care how you operate, as long as you do it efficiently. And as long as you don't get us involved in any criminal activity. I'm acting solely on Chloe's recommendation. Shall we talk price?"

We talked price. By the day, three hundred dollars for me and my partner, who had not yet arrived. Plus expenses, which would, since we were away from home, be considerable. She had no problems with my terms and I was sorry I hadn't asked for more.

I was looking her over carefully, without, I hoped, showing it. She was doing the same to me. I thought she was in
her late thirties, judging by the small wrinkles around her
eyes. Eyes which were trained assertively on my own as we
talked. She wanted me to understand that she was in charge.
That was all right with me, since she was, but her insistence
that I roll over under her gaze probably meant one of two
things: either she was a bit unsure of herself or she didn't
trust a man to take her position seriously. I decided to go for
the second option, at least for the time being.

I told her I knew the very rough outline of the story, but
needed some details.

"First of all," I began, "how did the thief get in?"

"Come with me." She got up and headed for the door. "I'll
show you."

I followed her along a hallway and down a back stairway
to the first floor, where she pushed open an unmarked door.
We entered a large room that contained at least a dozen file
cabinets, a table, and a chair. Over in a corner, a woman sat
at a desk typing file-folder labels. There was another door in
the wall to my right.

"This is the file room," Nora said unnecessarily, nodding a
greeting to the woman at the typewriter. "That's the window
they broke to get in." She pointed to a barred window. I
looked through the bars onto the same backyard I'd seen
from her office. A business on the first floor, apartment on
the second, small yellow car parked near the back door. I
stuck my face up against the bars and looked down. The
window was no more than four feet from the ground. "The
bars are new, since the break-in. Then they went into the
tank room and took everything back out through here, and
apparently out through the same window again. Because the
door to this room was still locked from the outside in the
morning."

"Tank room?"

"In there." She pointed toward the door I'd noticed earlier.

"Where was the broken glass?"

"Mostly on the inside."

"Who was the first person to come in here that morning?"

"I was."

"Did you notice any marks on the wall?"

"Not in here."

"What about outside?"

"A few scratches, I think."

"Where was the note?"

"Right here on the table."

"What about the security guard I saw downstairs? Wasn't there one here that night?"

She shook her head. "We didn't have one before the break-in. We've never been terribly concerned with security before. It's not that kind of town. At least we didn't think it was. I have to admit we're all feeling pretty nervous now." I could believe it. She was tense, like someone in a hurry. I remembered the receptionist's nervous glance at the guard.

"But you say this room is kept locked—and was, before the break-in?"

"Of course. This is not a public area. Confidentiality is very important in this field."

I could see I was going to have to learn more about her field. "But the door to the tank room—what is a tank room, anyway?—isn't kept locked?"

"The only way you can get to it is through this room. I'm afraid it never occurred to us that someone would come in the window."

Again, I asked, "What's the tank room?"

"That's where the sperm is stored." Once again, she led the way.

The room had no other doors and no windows. It was entirely bare except for half a dozen three-foot-tall objects that looked like heavy-duty milk cans. Each one had a number on it.

I walked over to the nearest one. "It looks like a milk can."

"Is that supposed to be a joke?" She was not amused. I wondered if she ever was.

"No. A creative observation. And the thieves just came in and opened this up . . ." I felt around the edges. "How does it open?"

She lifted the lid. A cloud of very cold vapor seeped out. Through the mist I could just make out a few long rods with numbered vials, each about the size of my little finger, attached to them. The rods were set in a rack that looked like it would hold a hundred times as many. She closed the lid again before I could get a better look.

"Those vials. Is the sperm in those?" She nodded.

"Frozen?"

She nodded again. "Hard as glass. In liquid nitrogen at minus one hundred ninety-six degrees centigrade. It's called cryopreservation."

"Like that cryo-something where they freeze people? So they can thaw them out when there's a cure for whatever killed them?"

"Yes. Suspended animation."

"Minus one ninety-six. Centigrade. I guess that's pretty cold. These tanks must be unique."

"Not really. They're just like the ones the cattle industry uses to store bull sperm."

And that, I thought, was also pretty cold. "How many samples can you store in one of these things?"

"A lot."

"And the few I saw in there?"

"Donated since the break-in." I took out my notebook and jotted down some of the information she'd given me. Then, since there wasn't anything else to see in the dim, chilly little room, we went back out.

"What's in these files?"

The woman who had been typing labels was painstakingly sticking them onto file folders.

"Donor information. Medical background, legal agreement. Each donor has a number for his file and his sample. Copies of donor profiles. That's how the recipients make their selections, by numbered donor profiles. No names. Just numbers. Totally anonymous."

"And the numbers on the cans?"

"They refer to the classifications—private rental storage, for example, or available to the public."

I nosed around the file room window for a while. One small scratch on the sill. Then I suggested we go back up to her office, sit down, and talk some more. She sighed. Clearly, I was taking too much of her time.

"Tell me this," I said as we walked up the steps. "Why would a guy do that? Donate?"

"Lots of reasons. Some men are donors for specific women. Some do it for the money. Twenty-five dollars. Some do it because they're starting cancer therapy or getting vasectomies or going to work at jobs where they may be exposed to chemical or radioactive mutagens."

We were settled in her office again. "Why is it frozen?"

She looked at me like I was an idiot. "So it will live long enough to be used."

I was not intimidated. "Could you elaborate?" I snapped.

She looked at me, startled. "Oh. I'm sorry. Of course. I'm afraid I'm distracted. There's so much work to do to make up for the damage. That break-in cost us a great deal of money."

I nodded kindly, and waited for her to go on.

"It's frozen for two reasons, really. Logistics, first of all. It can't live more than a day unfrozen. We store it for doctors and researchers as well as for private parties. Sometimes we ship it out of town, frozen. We rent the storage space to the doctors, and the researchers, and the men I mentioned before, who need to store their sperm for one reason or another. And to women with private donors. And of course we need to store a great deal of it, from a variety of donors, for the women who come here, the ones who want to have a child by an anonymous donor with no paternal rights." The words "over-the-counter sales" occurred to me. "Sometimes, two or three years down the line, a woman who's already had one child through us wants to have another one by the same donor." She must have noticed that I'd raised my eyebrows, because she added, "We can store, long-term, for up to seven years."

"Who are most of these women, I mean—"

"Most of them are women with infertile partners."

"How long has this been going on?"

"Well, if you mean insemination, that's been going on for a couple of centuries. But modern cryopreservation is relatively new—since the early sixties."

I made a few more general-interest notes and got back to more immediate matters. "And someone broke in and stole thousands and thousands of samples, took them out of the freezers—the tanks—and dumped them. Why?"

"We don't know. The police chief has the note they left, for all the good that will do, but I remember it word for word."

I nodded, holding my pen above a clean notebook page.

"It said, 'Godless destroyers of the family, be warned. We are setting free this seed in the ocean. Leave our town or suffer the consequences of your sins.' They spelled *consequences* wrong, with a C instead of a QU."

"Was it typewritten?"

"No. Messy block letters. Like someone had printed it with the hand they didn't usually use for writing."

I thought about that. It wasn't particularly smart to use a typewriter, because anyone who'd ever seen a movie knew that typewriter type was identifiable. But at the same time, anyone who'd ever seen a movie knew that the way to do a really bad note was with cut and paste letters. Maybe this guy, or group, was just too lazy to do it right.

I got up and walked to the window, looking once more at the back of the building across the way. "What's that shop over there?"

"Louis's Art Gallery and Bookstore."

"I have to say it seems a little odd that you'd have a sperm bank way out here instead of in San Francisco or the East Bay—somewhere closer to the center of things."

"We're considering opening another branch closer in. But actually, this is a very good location. We got a wonderful deal on the building. Safe neighborhood." She laughed, for the first time since I'd met her. It was a nice, rueful laugh. "We're reasonably central. Close enough to San Francisco, convenient to a number of large towns. Besides, I've tried living in the city. I want to live here. I was born here." She had stopped smiling. "And I don't plan to move."

—3—

Two phone calls and an "urgent" employee visit in the next fifteen minutes convinced me that Nora's absence on the job was beginning to be felt, so I didn't keep her more than half a dozen questions longer. I suggested we meet again that night, after I'd gotten to know the town better. She suggested, to my amazement, dinner at her place. I went back out onto the street with her address and directions on how to find it.

Nora had told me she didn't know of anyone who had openly declared themselves to be enemies of the bank, and had shrugged helplessly when I'd asked her if she'd gotten any bad feelings from anyone. She said she didn't have a lot of time to notice feelings, at least not at work.

I was beginning to understand the size of the crime. A great deal of money lost, yes. But what I couldn't get out of my head was the guys with cancer, and the ones with the poisonous jobs. A last chance at fatherhood, gone. I wondered how many attorneys had already started working on suits.

My next stops were the police station and the shop that had the most direct access to the bank's back windows. The shop first, because it was closer, and then the police.

Usually, when I'm on a case, I try to avoid all contact with the law, but I figured that wouldn't work very well in a town with a population of somewhere around two thousand. Not much chance I wouldn't be noticed, so I might as well be noticed right away.

I had my usual cover. A couple of years before, my old friend and poker buddy Artie Perrine, an editor at *Probe* magazine in San Francisco, had agreed to give me a letter of ID as a "freelance writer" on assignment. In exchange, I agreed to give him anything in the way of story material I might come up with while on a case. Chloe, who had gotten me involved in this one, was also an editor at *Probe*. Anyone who didn't believe the worn, yellowing, undated letter could just call the magazine for verification.

I have considered getting a P.I. license. It's hard to explain why I haven't been able to bring myself to do it. I guess I just don't like government very much and don't want it looking over my shoulder. Maybe it's genetic memory—a long history of fending off Slavic despots, Turkish soldiers, and Tatar hordes. I'd rather keep a low profile, thanks just the same.

The wind was whipping up a good one, full of horizontal rain, and this time I was walking into it. The art-shop sign was swinging hysterically, like a drenched man trying to flag a taxi. I allowed myself to be blown in the door.

A thin man with half a head of straight dark hair, sitting on a stool behind the register, looked up at me with a morose smile. The radio on the shelf behind him was delivering a weather report. At his feet was a half-unpacked cardboard carton of books, the return address a book distributor in San Francisco.

"Hi," he said. "I was just thinking about boarding up and going home. Can I help you?"

"Mind if I look around?"

He raised his shoulders and his eyebrows in resignation, still friendly, but clearly not expecting much from my presence except delay. I looked around.

The walls were covered with books, from worn linoleum floor to dingy ceiling, with two room-dividing partitions built out at right angles into the large room to hold paintings and drawings. There was one particularly nice series of charcoal drawings. Beach scenes, mostly, a few sketches of the town, and a portrait of the man who had been behind the counter and was now carrying sheets of plywood out of a back room. Except for a couple of watercolors that looked like they might have come from the same artist, the drawings were the only pieces in the gallery that looked anything like professional. There were some gummy-looking oils—a rowboat on the beach, a dune with wildflowers—that had to be the offspring of someone's Sunday hobby.

The books were mostly paperbacks, several sections of used books priced to sell, with one small table of California-published books on the ocean and the environs of Marin, Sonoma, and Mendocino counties. I figured those must be for the tourists.

The rain was battering the large front window and, as I passed near, it shuddered in the wind. Reluctantly, the dark-haired man leaned a sheet of plywood against the wall and followed me back to the register.

"I don't want to keep you long," I said, paying for a used

Parker mystery. "But I wonder if I could ask you a couple of questions."

"Short ones?" He was trying to stay pleasant. After all, I'd just spent fifty cents.

"Yeah. My name is Samson. Jake Samson. Are you Louis?"

"Yes. Lou Overman. This is my place."

"Do you live upstairs?"

"Why do you want to know?" His patience, like his hair, was wearing thin. I gave him the patter about being on assignment for *Probe* magazine, checking out the story on the burglary over at the sperm bank.

He nodded thoughtfully, gazing at me with interest, and admitted that he lived upstairs, although he failed to see what that had to do with the burglary. I didn't answer the implied question, just waited for him to get uncomfortable and say something else. He got uncomfortable fast.

"I guess it is a pretty strange story. Especially the part about dumping it in the ocean. Religious fanatics." He smiled wryly and looked sophisticated. I didn't see why the dumping was any stranger than the rest of the crime, but I smiled a world-weary smile to go with his sophisticated one.

I waved at the ceiling. "Your place must look out on the back of the bank, right? Where they broke in?"

The window shuddered again, and he glanced at his waiting plywood. "You could say it does."

"Let's. Did you see or hear anything that night?"

He made an effort to relax, leaning against his counter, looking sad. "No. I sleep soundly, I'm happy to say."

"No sound of glass breaking, no voices, no noise at all?"

He shook his head. "I didn't hear anything or see anything. Sorry." He glanced at the front window as it shuddered again.

I leaned against the counter and lowered my voice. "I was wondering, a businessman like yourself, you must know a lot of what goes on here in town. Maybe you've got some idea of who might have wanted to do a thing like this. Who in particular would disapprove of the kind of business they're running over there."

He responded well to his new status as an expert witness. "Tell you the truth, I don't know who it could be. Most of the people here are live-and-let-live types, pretty much. Oh, we have a few people who take their religion too seriously, and a few rednecks, like everywhere else, but"—he shook his head—"I can't imagine who would actually do something like that." He gave me a sharp look from suddenly clear dark eyes. "But I can keep my eyes and ears open if you want me to—and maybe if you let me know some of the things you find out, I can help you put two and two together."

I got a powerful feeling that his next words were going to have something to do with either his private detecting fee or a mention of his shop in my article, so I thanked him, said I hoped he would keep his ear to the ground, said that his big plate glass window was really taking a beating and it looked like maybe he'd better cover it real quick, and said I would be talking to him again. Then I flipped the slicker hood back over my head, smiled at him in a way that I hoped promised rewards of some kind to come, and struggled out onto the sidewalk again. What there had been of late-afternoon sunlight was fading.

The gutter would have been a good spot for whitewater rafting, and it was only a matter of time, I thought, before the sidewalks would be washed by waves from the street traffic. If there was any. I was getting worried about the roads. Rosie Vicente, my partner, friend, sometime carpenter, and tenant at my two-cottage Oakland place, was due to arrive that evening. I'd already reserved a room for her at the Oceanview, where they said they didn't mind renting to a woman with a polite, middle-aged standard poodle.

Rosie's dog, Alice B. Toklas, is a sophisticated traveler

who spends most of her time sleeping in the car. I have never tried traveling with my cats, Tigris and Euphrates, and never will. They were now in the care of a sitter.

I had hoped, on this first ramble through the town, to get a feel for it and for its people. But the people were not outside where they could be seen, and every time I raised my eyes to look around I got leaves and twigs and rain in the face. So I plodded, head down, to the police station.

The cop behind the desk was in his early sixties, I guessed, a gray man with gray hair and watery gray eyes. His small feet were propped up on the desk, and his reading matter of choice was *TV Guide*.

He looked surprised when I stumbled in, dripping, smiling like a friendly idiot.

His radio, like everyone else's, was tuned to a weather report. I heard something about fifty-mile-an-hour winds.

I threw back my hood, unzipped the front of the slicker, strode purposefully up to his desk, stuck out my hand, and told him my name. His, he said, was Clement Paisley, a name which I thought suited him not at all. Chief Clement Paisley.

He asked me to take a seat. The only seat, besides the wooden bench under the front window, was a sprung secretarial chair, but I took it. With a soft thunk it dropped a notch on its shaft.

I told him I was interested in learning more about the problem over at the sperm bank for a possible article in *Probe* magazine.

"*Probe*," he said. "I've seen it on the stands somewhere. Never read it. San Francisco, right? So, you work in San Francisco." For some reason, he thought that was amazing.

"I'm a freelancer," I said. Which was true, as far as it went.

"So I guess you live down there?"

"Oakland."

"I got a boy lives in Berkeley. Well, not exactly a boy. He's thirty-six this year. About your age, I guess?"

"About." Not quite.

He shook his head. "I don't know how anybody can live down there. What exactly is it you're interested in finding out, Mr. Samson?"

"Well, for a start, I hear you found the stolen items on the beach."

"Not on the beach, exactly, and only some of them, floating around, up against the rocks. Most of them must have been washed out to sea. Would have been."

"So you're the person who found them?"

"Well, how it worked was Nora saw what had happened and called over here. I went to have a look. Saw the note, went to the beach. There was a kid out there, young boy from town. He was there already. Said he'd seen all that stuff in the water, didn't know what it was. So I guess you could say he found it. He kind of hung around while we hauled out the evidence, or what was left of it. You ever write anything besides magazine pieces?"

"Sometimes. Why?" I never write anything at all except an occasional letter to my father in Chicago.

"Oh, I don't know. I've been thinking about retirement lately—it's not so far off now. I've seen a lot in my day. A whole lot." He squinted at me appraisingly. "Thought I might try my hand at some detective stories sometime. Maybe use a partner who knows some of the ins and outs of the writing game."

"Interesting idea," I said, looking very interested. "Maybe we can talk about that some more when I've finished my story here. We might have a pretty good mystery going right now." A man with delusions of fictional wealth could be useful, particularly since he was thinking I might be useful to him. For once, maybe, I wouldn't have to spend my time toe-dancing around the sensibilities of the law, with its peculiar idea that maybe someone should arrest me for withholding information—which I do not do—or interfering with an investigation, which is a pretty fuzzy charge as far as I'm concerned.

Paisley startled me by laughing a Mike Hammer kind of laugh. "Not much of a mystery, if you ask me. Just a prank. Kids, probably. I got a lot of things to do around here that take priority over a prank. We got people growing dope in the hills. We got a wifebeater or two. We got some mean drunks. And it looks like we're going to be having some flooding problems if this keeps up." He cast a countryman's weather eye toward the window—self-consciously, I thought. After all, northern California may be country but it's not Indiana.

"It's funny," I said conversationally. "I guess city people just don't think of you folks up here having crime problems. But of course you do. I can see you've got a tough job." I had gone just an inch too far. He looked at me suspiciously.

"That's right. Nothing like Oakland, of course, but it would take an army to handle things there."

I agreed. "In the meantime, though, I really need to check out this sperm bank thing. That's what my editors are interested in, and I'm a workingman. The ins and outs of the writing game. I wonder if I could have a look at the note the vandals left."

"Sure," he said, one workingman to another. "You can have a look at it."

"Actually, what I'd like is a copy—maybe for reproduction in the magazine."

"Only copy machine is over at the drugstore. I'll see if I can't get my man to run over and make a copy later, but we're going to be pretty busy."

"I could run it over there myself."

Maybe he thought the break-in was just a prank, but he was enough of a cop not to let evidence go drifting off with a stranger. He gave me a sly smile.

"I think you know I can't do that, Mr. Samson." He laughed. "You're a tricky one."

I smiled back at him. I was beginning to enjoy his company. He chuckled again, got up, and went into a back room. He returned with a plastic bag. The note was in it. He smoothed the plastic on the desk and let me look.

It was exactly as Nora Canfield had said, complete with "Godless destroyers" and the misspelled "consecenses."

I looked closely at the printing. Made with a soft pencil. Very laboriously done, very unstable-looking. The lines were wavy, the verticals and horizontals were neither vertical nor horizontal, exactly. The lines slanted downward on the unlined, cheap typing paper. The kind of paper you could buy at the local drugstore when you went to make copies of whatever it was you made copies of.

I agreed with Nora. The printing looked a lot like it was done by someone using the wrong hand. Or some senile crazy. Or some barely literate and not too well coordinated kid.

I thanked Chief Paisley.

"Tell me this," I said. "You think the whole thing was just a prank. Why is that? It looks pretty serious to me on the face of it. Even if you just think in terms of the money that's been lost."

"Oh, I know the people in this town, Mr. Samson. There may be one or two who might write something like this, but they're not the kind who could pull off a burglary, or lug cases of what they stole all the way to Spicer Street Beach, if they did decide to do such a peculiar thing."

"Who might those people be?"

He frowned and shook his head. "I'm not going to send you around to scare innocent people. But I'll tell you this—two of them are too old and one of them's too young, and a cripple to boot."

"Do you know of anyone who might have it in for Nora herself? Does she have any enemies?"

"None that I know of."

"No one besides a disabled kid and a couple of old people who might be angry that she set up that kind of shop in their town? No one who might want to scare her off?"

"I can't see anyone caring about any of that. This town gets most of its money from tourists, after all. Whatever reason people have for coming here, they're just more customers for the restaurants and shops and motels. Sure, maybe some people grumble, but nothing big."

"Are you sure someone broke in—that the thieves really used the window, and didn't have a key to the door?"

"You mean did someone fake all that window stuff, breaking it and so forth?"

"Yes."

"I'm pretty sure. Glass on the inside, on the floor. Scratches on the outside wall and the sill. No reason to believe it was an inside job." He smirked when he said the last two words, like he enjoyed using them and making fun of them at the same time.

"I was just wondering if there might not be someone working at the bank who—"

"You probably ought to ask Nora that one." The phone rang. It seemed very loud, even with the wind carrying on outside. He picked it up. I looked out the window. Nearly dark. A sheet of rain washed the glass; I couldn't see through it at all.

"Well, hello, Melody, how are you?" Pause. "Uh-huh. It doesn't look too awfully good. I'm going to have to send Perry out to take a look . . . right. We'll keep on top of it, so try not to worry too much." Pause. "Well, whatever you think. Maybe we'll see you, then." He hung up.

"Lady's got a house out on the spit," he said. "Line of big houses out there, built right out into the water. Pretty high up, but you never can tell when it blows this way."

"Does she want you to hold her hand?" I asked.

He laughed. "She doesn't live out there in the winter. She's a big writer down in San Francisco. Real celebrity. Just keeping tabs on her real estate."

An elderly woman fought her way in the door, swathed from head to foot in transparent plastic.

"Angie!" Paisley was happily surprised. "I didn't expect you to come back here tonight."

She smiled at him, her face pink and pleased. "I thought that with the weather and all you might need some help."

"Well, that's just wonderful. Make yourself some tea and then see if you can get Perry on the radio."

She retired into a back room, dripping water from every pleat and fold.

I brought him back to my case. "Did you find anything besides the note—anything that might give you some lead?"

He shook his head. "They busted in, emptied the freezers, got away clean."

"Clement?" It was the elderly woman calling from the back room.

"Yes, Angie?"

"Perry says he's just going to get himself some supper, then he'll go on out to the spit like you asked."

Paisley made a face. "He eats too much." Then he stood up. "I better take a quick ride around town, see if everything's holding together all right." He reached for a long black raincoat hanging from an aluminum coatrack that looked like it had been rejected by a cheap cafeteria. "Want to come with me?" He was talking to me.

"No, thanks," I replied. "Maybe some other time."

He laughed. "I didn't think reporters minded getting a little damp. Maybe we can have a beer together sometime, talk some more about those detective books. Meanwhile, long as I'm out, I'll make a copy of this for you." He waved the plastic-enclosed note at me, then stuck it in his raincoat pocket.

—4—

I didn't see any reason to think that the chief had the right idea about the break-in at the bank, or that he was even telling me what he really thought. For all I knew, he was frying fish I couldn't even smell. He belonged to the town. Just because he seemed friendly and open, just because he was on the verge of retirement and acted countrified, just because his office help looked like my third-grade teacher back in more innocent times—none of that meant anything. I had wandered through these parts in my younger years. Behind every redwood tree, every rock on the beach, lurks wary sophistication. Too many refugees from San Francisco had come this way. Too many artists and gays and entrepreneurs had moved in to stay.

Maybe Paisley had managed to remain unwise in the ways of the real world, but I figured I'd reserve judgment, and keep right on thinking that there were some very nasty people living in this small and pretty town.

I wanted to stop in at a local tavern and chat around, and maybe hit one or two other spots on the main strip, but my pants legs were soaked below the thigh-length slicker and my waterproofed boots weren't working so well anymore. I could barely see where I was going, and with the wind at my front I felt like that guy in mythology who has to keep pushing a boulder uphill for all eternity. Which is better than feeling like the man whose liver is being eaten by a big bird, but not by much.

I leaned into the wind and worked my way back to the motel, wondering the whole way whether Rosie was going to be able to make it up here at all in the next day or two. Some of the roads north all but disappeared when the weather was bad enough. Of course, I had no idea how widespread the storm was, or how much rain had fallen. A lot, I knew that.

So I was pretty damned happy to see Rosie's pickup in the motel parking lot. Not only was she safe, she was here early.

I checked with the man at the desk and he told me she had the room next to mine.

"By the way, Mr. Samson," he added, "it's all right, of course, but you did say she had a small dog."

"No I didn't," I objected. "I said she had a standard poodle."

"Oh. I thought you said 'your standard poodle,' you know. A regular little fluffball. That dog has to weigh eighty pounds. I didn't know there was such a thing. You mean that's really a poodle?"

"Yes." I tried to get away.

"I'll be damned. Smart dog, I'll bet. Well, I like dogs, just as long as he doesn't make a mess—"

"She's a she. And she weighs seventy pounds. Thanks for being so understanding. I'm kind of wet and I'd like to see my friend."

He raised his hands in a don't-let-me-stop-you gesture, and I stepped out of the puddle I had been making in front of his desk.

I went to Rosie's room first, and knocked. Alice whined quietly in greeting, and Rosie opened the door. She was wrapped in a big purple terry-cloth robe and her short dark hair was wet.

"I'm glad you came up early," I said. I noticed our rooms had a connecting door. "I'm going to go get dried off a bit, then we can talk. Looks like you got wet too."

"Just a little," she said wryly. "You know that spot on 101 in San Rafael?"

"The part that floods?"

"Uh-huh. It had, and that was where I got the flat tire. Fortunately, I did get an early start. The storm's not going to let up tonight and I was afraid I wouldn't be able to get through at all."

"I'm glad you did. We've got an interesting one this time."

I went to my own room, toweled myself dry, and put on fresh clothes. Dry socks helped a lot. I knocked on the connecting door.

Rosie had had the foresight to stop somewhere and get a six-pack of beer, remarkable foresight, I thought, under the circumstances. She was dressed, now, in a sweater and corduroy pants. The bulk of her clothing didn't conceal the strength or the softness of a body that turned the heads of various genders. Not spectacular, mind you, but very tidy. We cracked a couple of the beers and I told her what we had so far. Which reminded me that Nora was expecting one person for dinner, not two and a dog. I dialed the home number she'd given me and left a message on her answering machine. Then I got back to our discussion of the case.

"Where do you think we should start?" Rosie wanted to know.

"With some hip boots," I groused. I turned on Rosie's transistor radio. Sure enough, more weather. A big ugly front out over the Pacific.

I left the radio on low. "We need to get to know the people in this town. We need to check out the religious fanatics the chief mentioned. We need to talk to the kid who found the stuff at the beach before Paisley got there. Oh, hell, you know. We need to be able to walk through town without using oars."

"What time's dinner?"

I told her.

"We've got a while, then. We could spend some time in a local tavern, catching the gossip."

That's one of the things I love about working with Rosie. We think alike.

Still, I wasn't eager to go out into the storm again.

"Let's finish these beers first, okay? It's dry in here."

"You're such a tough guy, Jake."

"Never said I was. Never will say so. People start expecting tough, a guy could get hurt."

We both remembered a few times when the guy had, indeed, gotten hurt.

"Okay, so what we're dealing with is several different possibilities."

"Right."

"It's a prank, like the chief says. It's the work of someone with religious convictions. It's someone trying to get to Nora or to her company and covering up their real motives."

"Right." I finished my beer and stood up, ready to go again. "Or it's something else."

— **5** —

It was still raining, but not quite as hard, and the wind had died down somewhat. According to the Chevy's radio, though, the lull was just that and the storm was going to have plenty more to offer before the night was over.

I remembered seeing a tavern not far from the police station. It was certainly not the only one in town, but at least I knew where it was. We parked on the street, right in front of an antique store with plywood nailed over its display window. The grocery store on the other side of the tavern was still open, and its smaller window was uncovered.

Henry's Pub, pretentious though its name might be, was a pleasant, dimly lighted place with real wood paneling and a scarred and ancient bar. The few patrons, I suspected, were regulars who were not deterred by weather. A couple of guys who looked like hard drinkers perched on stools at the bar. A leftover hippie was playing pinball, and a man and woman in their forties huddled at a tiny table looking like they didn't have much to say to each other but hoped that being out in public would help.

The bartender had a neat red beard and short red hair and a square face saved from Prussian sternness by soft brown eyes. Rosie and I grabbed a couple of stools.

"Hi. What can I get you?" A friendly, sad smile. We ordered beers. He slid them across the bar to us. "Visiting?" We said yes. "Not a real nice day for it."

"We noticed," I agreed. "And it sounds like it's going to get worse."

"Bad enough, but not too bad, maybe. Not like last year." The winter before, whole towns had been flooded out in Sonoma county. "Weather service says it'll blow by, tomorrow sometime."

He didn't seem terribly concerned. "People seem to think," I said, "that there'll be some property damage."

"Maybe. Mostly out on the spit, and those folks are insured up the ying-yang."

"I heard some of those houses are owned by celebrities."

He leaned a little closer. The subject interested him. "Ever hear of Melody Clift? Marty Spiegel?"

"Melody Clift?" Rosie perked up. "Isn't she a writer? Romance novels or something like that?" I was amazed. I would never expect Rosie to recognize the name of a romance novelist. Come to think of it, though, the name did sound familiar. "And Spiegel," Rosie continued, "he's the movie director. Big." She turned to me. "You know, Jake, he did *Pirates of the Martian Sea.*"

I knew, all right. Everyone did.

"'Course neither of them's in town right now," the bartender said. "Melody's in and out, but Spiegel—he spends most of his time in L.A., I guess."

The conversation lagged for a beat or two, and it seemed like a good time to introduce a new subject.

"I hear you had some other excitement around here a couple of days ago."

He half-smiled. "Oh, yeah. You must mean the break-in over at the bank."

One of the drunks halfway down the bar snickered. The other one said, "Hey, Wolf, how about another bullshot?"

Wolf—Wolf?—brought the man another bullshot. I ordered another beer to bring him back to our end of the bar.

"I'd think a crime that big would be quite an event out here," I said.

Wolf shook his head. "Bunch of kids. Big joke."

"The people at the bank don't think it's too funny."

The laughing drunk laughed louder. "Guess this guy's a depositor. You got an account over there, fella?" He cracked himself up. Wolf gave him a disgusted look, and the drunk tried to stop grinning.

"Got any particular set of kids in mind?" I asked.

He studied my face. "You some kind of insurance investigator or something?"

"No. I don't even believe in the stuff. Insurance, I mean."

He moved down the bar to talk to the drunks, which only goes to show how little he wanted to talk to us. Rosie was meditating quietly over her beer. I figured she'd start to ask some questions once she got her bearings in the town.

Right about then a tall fat man came in, shedding rivers from his Christmas-tree-green plastic coat. When he walked closer to the bar, I recognized the white-faced man from the café, the one whose house on the spit had been an object of amusement to his buddy. His face looked even paler, almost gray, like a dead man's.

"Hey, Henry," Wolf said, looking surprised. "What are you doing back here so quick?"

Henry leaned over the bar, took Wolf's shoulders in his hands, and said something to him softly. Wolf's body sagged, and his face looked like it was melting. The big man let go of him just long enough to get his body around and behind the bar. He led the bartender out to a chair.

The old hippie, the man and woman, and the two drunks surrounded Wolf and his large nurse.

"Hey, man," the old hippie whined. "What's goin' on? What was that about Gracie?"

"Drowned," Henry said. "She was out at the spit and it looks like she got blown over or slipped or something. Down onto the rocks. Maybe a wave took her. That's all I know. Listen, Wolf, you go along home."

Wolf shook his head. "Rather be here."

"I'm your boss. Do what I say. My place, I say who works the bar and who goes home."

"Fuck you." Wolf continued to sit rigidly in his chair.

"Okay." Henry backed off. "But you just sit there." He peeled off his still-dripping coat and squeezed back behind the bar. Rosie ordered another beer.

Except for the bored couple, the other patrons of the bar drifted away from Wolf uneasily, the bearded time-warp back to his pinball, the drunks back to their drinks. The couple sat down with him, offering a kind of silent condolence. Wolf jumped to his feet. "I'm going to go find out what happened."

Henry opened his mouth to object, then closed it again. The couple, their first overture rejected, watched Wolf go without offering to go with him.

Henry stared at the door. "Bad luck," he sighed. "You'd think he'd have had enough of that."

"This hit him pretty hard," Rosie said. "Who was Gracie to him, anyway?"

"Girlfriend. They been dating for a couple years. Going to get married."

"Rough," I said. "I guess she lived out there on the spit, then?"

He shook his head. "No. I don't know what the hell she was doing out there in this weather."

"So," Rosie pursued, "he's had a lot of bad luck?"

Henry ignored the question and went down the bar to fill another order.

I looked at my watch. It was 7:45. We were due at Nora's at 8:00.

Alice was curled up on the backseat of the Chevy. She roused herself to greet us, then flopped back down again. She wasn't even going to bother to look out the window as she rode. Smart dog. There was nothing to see. We checked Nora's directions. Her house was in the hills overlooking the town.

—6—

Class and social lines are drawn clearly in a town like Wheeler, as much now as in the past. Maybe more now, with its mix of urban immigrants and old residents. The lines are drawn by nature and by the way that people see it—literally.

The very rich who were new to the town lived out on the spit, right out in the ocean, but above it. Close to its power but superior, like gods.

I hadn't seen much of the side streets yet, but I was willing to bet that most of them were made up of homes for lower- and middle-income people, many of whom had been there for static generations. On some of those side streets, I knew, old mansions still rested in their spacious gardens, built by Victorians who were more interested in creating their own splendor than in looking at the ocean from their living room windows. Some of those might still be occupied by old families. Some would have been converted to inns. Some would have been cut up into flats.

The hills at the edge of town, on the other hand, held the newer construction of those who had some money, were priced out of the spit but wanted a view of the ocean. Successful people who could afford better than the viewless heart of town. People like Nora.

The rain had evened off to a steady downpour, and the road we took up into the hills, narrow and winding, was hard to negotiate. Parts of it were half-buried in slide debris and slippery with mud. Her house was set snugly among shrubs and partly sheltered by a good-sized black locust tree. The size of the tree told me that the house was probably about twenty years old, an A-frame modification of redwood and glass. Small, but I was betting she had a nice view of the Pacific from that upstairs room.

When Nora answered the door she asked if the dog was okay with cats. We assured her that Alice was very fond of cats, and we were all allowed in.

She offered us wine, and we sat down in a comfortable, small living room with a big stone fireplace warming and cheering and sending fragrant hardwood smoke up the chimney. Soft, deep chairs. The rug was a reasonable dark color, so it didn't matter too much if Alice's paws were damp and possibly muddy. I relaxed fully for the first time that day, sipped the wine, listened to the Vivaldi she'd put on the stereo. She was in the kitchen, working on something that smelled of curry. Rosie was in there, too, checking out the food. I just sat, wanting nothing more than warmth and dryness.

They came back into the living room. Nora looked distressed.

"I was just telling her what we heard about that woman who fell off the cliff," Rosie said.

"It was an accident? Is that what you heard?"

A small knife of guilt cut me. "I'm sorry. We should have said something right away. You know her, then?" Of course she did. In a town this size?

"It had to be Gracie Piedmont. She's been seeing Wolf. And you heard it was an accident?"

"Sounded that way," I said. "Why?"

"I'm sure it must have been," she said softly. "There's no reason why it would have anything to do with the break-in. But it seems so odd . . ."

Her reaction was dragging me out of my warm stupor. A gray cat strolled out of the kitchen, made itself big and fuzzy, arched its back, and glared at Alice, who wagged her tail tentatively.

"Why would it have anything to do with the break-in?" Rosie wanted to know.

"Well, she worked with us. She was an employee."

The cat continued to glare at Alice, who sighed and closed her eyes.

I sighed, too, and stood up. "How do we get to the spit?"

"Why?"

Rosie explained. "It probably doesn't have anything to do with what happened at the bank. It was probably just an accident. But if there's any chance that there is a connection, we need to go out there and see if there's anything to see before everything's taken away. Or washed away."

"Of course," Nora said, her incomprehension replaced by resolution. "Let me get a coat and turn off the oven. I'll come too."

I told her that wasn't necessary, but she wouldn't listen. We put our coats back on. Alice dragged herself away from the fire.

On the way down the hill, over that rotten road again, we asked Nora a few questions about the dead woman. She was in her early thirties. She had worked at the sperm bank. She had lived in Wheeler all her life and had relatives in town.

"What kind of job did she have?" Rosie asked.

"Mostly bookkeeping. But she also helped out part-time with insemination. Instructing women who do it at home, working at the clinic with women who want to do it there. A lot of us wear a number of hats. We try not to pigeonhole our employees."

Just as I turned onto the road that led out onto the spit, an ambulance passed us going the other way. I aimed at a cluster of vehicles huddled in the flashing lights of two police cars, about halfway out. Not much of a road. Straight enough from land side to point, but barely paved and chuckholed, flooded six inches deep in places, with a film of mud, washing out of the lots above, smearing the surface. Through the rain and the trees I could just make out a few houses at the upper side of the road. At our left, nothing but grass, mud, and rock ending suddenly about twenty-five yards from the road.

From what I could see of the houses, they were big. There didn't seem to be very many of them, but there could have been others tucked farther back in the trees. I had no idea how wide the spit might be, but it was no more than five hundred yards long.

Besides the two police cars, there were a big old station wagon and a county car. A solitary figure squatted out in the rain and wind on the grassy bluff overlooking the ocean.

I pulled up alongside the wagon. Paisley was sitting inside, in the passenger seat. I couldn't see who was behind the wheel. I rolled down my window; the chief rolled down his.

He jerked a thumb at the backseat of the Chevy, where Alice, her large body obscuring Nora, was peering through the glass. "Funny-looking bloodhound you got there."

"Heard there was an accident, Clement."

He opened his door, slid out, and ducked into the backseat of the Chevy with Alice and Nora. The wagon's driver slid across the front seat to get a better look at us. It was a woman, swathed in clear plastic.

"How'd you find out?" Paisley demanded.

"My partner and I"—I introduced him to Rosie—"were in Henry's when he came in to tell Wolf."

Paisley sighed. "Yeah. Wolf came running out here. We sent him home."

"Who's that?" I asked, nodding at the woman in the wagon.

"Dead woman's cousin. Fredda Carey."

"What happened?" Rosie asked.

"Hard to tell. That's the coroner's man out there sitting in the mud." He was referring to the figure I'd seen out on the edge. "Looks like she slipped down the bank, maybe got caught by a wave and pulled over." He glanced quickly at the cousin and whispered, "Onto the rocks. All battered up."

The cousin didn't miss the whisper. She got out of the wagon, swinging cheap plastic boots, muddied to the ankle, down onto the wet road, and came over to join us, standing wretchedly in the rain.

"Hello, Nora," she said, glancing into the backseat. Then, to Paisley, "Who are these people?" He introduced Rosie and me as magazine writers from San Francisco.

Nora leaned around the dog. "They just told me, Fredda. I'm very sorry." The woman acknowledged the condolence with a heavy shrug.

The door of the other police car slammed, and a young cop trudged over to us. He was the one I had seen at the café that afternoon, the one who looked out for other people's investments. He mumbled something to Paisley about the morgue, and Angie, and the radio. "Okay, Perry," the chief said.

There were a lot of questions I wanted to ask Paisley, but that was hard to do with the cousin, and everyone else, clustered in and around the car. I invited him to step across the road with me. Out in the rain again, I walked him across the grass toward the coroner's man. Rosie stayed with the others.

"Where's the body?" I began.

"Ambulance been and gone. Some job, hauling her up off those rocks."

"What was she doing out here? And what's her cousin doing out here? Does the Carey woman live on the spit?"

He snorted. "Not much chance of that. No, see what happened was Fredda and Gracie were having dinner together at Gracie's, when this friend of Gracie's called. Marty Spiegel, his name is. Heard of him?" I nodded. "Anyway, he called and he was sitting down there in L.A. and getting all worried about his house up here in the storm. Asked her to go out and take a look, give him a call back."

"When was that?"

"Around five, a little past. Just dark. By six she wasn't back yet and Fredda got worried, gave me a call. That was right about the time Perry was getting out there to check on things. I had Angie relay the message to his car. He actually spotted the body down on the rocks. Must have done some real work for a change."

"Then you came out here?"

He nodded.

"And you called the cousin?"

"No. She called the station a while later. We knew Gracie was dead by then. Angie told Fredda we'd found her, Fredda came on out."

"When was that?"

"About an hour ago."

I looked at my watch. It was a quarter to nine. "When did Wolf get here?"

"About fifteen minutes after Fredda." That tallied with the time he'd left the bar.

The coroner's man slogged across the grass and joined us.

"What do you think, Kurt?" Paisley asked.

The man laughed and shook his head. "Could have slipped. Could be one of those waves came up over the top. There's some rock dislodged, but there's nothing much to see, all this rain still coming down."

I broke in. "Could she have been pushed?"

The man looked at me as though he'd just seen me turn purple. Paisley introduced me, and Kurt grunted. "Looks to me like she just got too close to the edge." He smirked. "Of course, if she was poisoned or shot or anything, the autopsy ought to show it. I'll give you a call tomorrow or so, Clement." He drifted off. A couple of minutes later I heard the county car start. The lights went on and he swung around and headed back down the road.

I walked closer to the edge and looked down. Not very high up, after all. Maybe twenty-five or thirty feet to the rocks below, a scene like the inside of an overeager washing machine with a dozen agitators. A wave battered the rocks, washing over them. Another, higher wave crashed halfway up the scarp. The wind was trying to push me away from the edge, and I should have let it. I had to leap back when a third, much larger wave lunged at the spit, gobbling it up to the lip, spraying me with foam, turning my mud-plastered boots into soaked sponges and my pants legs into dishrags.

"I don't think I'd stand out there if I were you," Clement said. I rejoined him on more solid ground.

"I don't get it," I said. "The house is back there in the trees, right?" He nodded. "Then what the hell was she doing out here on the edge in this weather?"

He shrugged. "Does seem a little peculiar. But people get killed along this coast all the time. Don't take a storm serious enough. Don't take the ocean serious enough, for that matter. People do stupid things. You just did." He began to walk back toward the cars. I followed him, but I wasn't finished with our talk. Perry, Rosie, Nora, and Fredda were all sitting in the Chevy. Clement headed that way, but I cut him off, asking for a few more minutes alone.

For the first time, I noticed the tail end of an old white Gremlin sticking out of an overgrown driveway across the road.

"Is that the house?" I asked as we climbed into Clement's warm, dry car.

"Yeah. And that's Gracie's car."

"Any way to tell if there was any violence?"

"She was all banged up. Head. Body. Probably won't be any way to tell a thing like that."

"What about the car? Anything there?"

"No. No blood, if that's what you mean."

"Any sign of a second person?"

"You mean like a puddle on the floor of the passenger side?"

I smiled. "Exactly."

He smiled back. "You sure you've never done any detective stories? I'll tell you, Perry didn't look for anything like that—you wouldn't need a low-paying job, would you?—but I checked it out. I thought about another car, too, but hell, fifteen minutes of this rain would have washed away any sign of that. No way to show this was anything but an accident."

"Clement," I said, but the name was swallowed in a sudden gust that pushed at the patrol car and drowned it in a wash of rain. "Clement, you've had two violent events here in less than a week. A break-in, with destruction of valuable property, and now a death. And the dead woman worked for the place that got burglarized."

He shifted irritably in his seat. "Don't argue with me, Jake, and don't lecture me. I'm wet and I'm tired and a woman I've known all her life . . . look, I don't disagree with you." Car doors slammed. I rolled down my window to see what was going on. Perry was getting into his car, Fredda Carey into hers. She started the engine and drove away. I rolled the window up again.

"Sorry, Clement. Go ahead."

"Like I said, I don't disagree with you. But I still think the break-in was a prank, and even if I think this needs looking into, a little physical evidence would be a big help in getting started. Maybe, with something to go on, I could get some help from the sheriff. He wasn't too impressed about the break-in." He sighed. "Then again, maybe he's more ready for pasture than I am, and doesn't get too impressed with anything anymore."

"You're not ready for pasture." Despite my wariness of lawmen, I was beginning to like the man, and I didn't like hearing him put himself down.

He laughed and patted my shoulder. "You're a nice fellow, Jake. Maybe I could get put out to stud."

I didn't know what to say to that, so I told him I wanted to get a quick look at the dead woman's car. He said he'd open it up for me, but I couldn't touch anything.

Rosie saw where we were going and hopped out of the Chevy. The three of us crossed to the driveway. We looked around the Gremlin. No tracks of any kind on the smooth paving. I walked up the drive, looking to either side. No marks on the grass, no footprints, a lot of leaves and debris lying around from the storm.

Nothing I could see in the car.

The lights of a tow truck were coming down the road.

Driving back off the spit, I noticed that the visible houses had boarded-up windows, and reflected that at least some of the residents believed in being prepared.

Unfortunately, there wasn't much I could do to prepare for that drive, again, up into the hills. The road was even worse. I drove very slowly while we talked about the events of the night. Rosie said that Fredda had elaborated on what happened, somewhat, to Nora. The two cousins had been drinking wine. Not much, Fredda had insisted. And Marty Spiegel had called and asked Gracie if she could possibly go out and check on his house. She had told Fredda to sit tight and listen to the stereo and she'd be right back. An hour later Fredda called the police. She called again, a bit more than an hour after that, to learn from Angie that Perry had found Gracie and Clement had gone out to the spit. That was when Fredda had driven there.

"She kept blaming herself for not getting worried sooner, not going out to see what was wrong," Nora said. "They grew up together."

"You didn't by any chance ask her why her cousin might have walked out on a cliff in the middle of a gale?" I asked as I maneuvered, with some relief, into the driveway.

"I did mention that. She said something about Gracie being a romantic. That she liked storms. Then she just broke down and said she had to go pick up her daughter."

The curried chicken was badly dried out, but we ate it anyway. Nora tossed our socks into the dryer, and I toweled my pants legs as well as I could. The dog had settled again by the fire, but the cat was keeping its distance.

"What do you think, Nora?" I asked. "Was Gracie a romantic? Or was she just suicidal?"

She thought about it. "I don't really know. She was a nice person, quiet. A good employee. Steady. I always liked her, but she was younger than I am, so we didn't go to school together or anything. Nice. A good worker. We didn't have a lot in common. She didn't have any, well, drive. . . ."

Her tone was not exactly patronizing, but it was clear that she had seen nothing in Gracie but a good, pliable flunky. Nora had by this time drunk a good deal of wine, and was beginning to relax.

"Could she have had anything to do with the break-in?" I sipped the cold wine and took a last bite of chicken. Sawdust.

"Do you mean did she do it? Would she do it?"

"Well? Would she?"

To my surprise, she laughed. "I think she'd be more likely to fall off a cliff."

I changed the subject; I didn't much like hearing her talk

about this one. "I was wondering something. You said you have strict rules of confidentiality. Does that mean that only a few employees work in that section?"

She nodded. "For the sake of confidentiality and as a precaution against error. The last thing you want to do with a man's frozen sperm is get it mixed up with someone else's. Get the records switched or something. These things are all carefully cross-referenced, and we can't have some new employee fumbling around in there."

"Who does fumble around in there, then?" Rosie asked.

Nora smiled. "I do. And one woman who has access to all the records, and is in charge of them." She looked at me. "You saw her there this afternoon." I remembered. The woman who was typing labels.

"But not Gracie Piedmont?" I asked.

"No."

"Was she really friends with Marty Spiegel?"

"I believe so."

"Just friends?"

"I wouldn't know."

"How did they meet?"

"At the bank." She bit her lip. She hadn't meant to say that. Her face closed down, her usual tension returned, and Rosie, ever alert, turned to less confidential matters.

"So," she said. "How's business? I mean before all the trouble happened."

"Business was great, and it is again. Or will be."

"Big future in this kind of thing?"

She smiled smugly at Rosie. "There are currently something like twenty thousand children conceived every year in the United States by our method."

Darn, I thought, I never get in on the ground floor.

—7—

By the time we left Nora's that night, the storm had kicked up several notches to a full-force gale. Getting to the car, ten feet down the driveway, was like swimming a wild river upstream. Rosie held on to Alice's collar the whole way, pulling the horrified and half-drowned animal along, yanking open the car door and giving her a boost inside.

Nora had invited us to stay the night, but I wanted to get back to the privacy of our motel and work some things through.

The road was hellish. My ancient windshield wipers, never particularly speedy, were nearly useless, and I had to roll the side window down to see anything at all. At one point I had to guide the Chevy through mud and rock that must have been a foot deep, washed down from the hill above. That was on the easy part, where the road was sheltered somewhat by trees. A dangerous kind of shelter, with those big eucalyptuses tossing their heads like 1968 schoolgirls, but shelter, nevertheless. I crept down the hill and around a hairpin curve, remembering that there were exposed places where the ground fell away steeply below the road, and where the wind, much worse now than on any of our previous trips up and down, would be coming off the ocean right at us. We hit one, suddenly and sooner than I thought we would, and got belted by a blast that wrenched the wheel out of my hands and nearly smashed us into a rock wall. Nearly.

It took me twenty minutes to hit the main street and what I hoped was the safety of the motel. I parked as close to the shelter of the building as I could get. The lot was strewn with branches. I was thinking I should have asked for more money for this job.

We went to our rooms to get dry and changed. I wiped the mud off my boots and left them sitting near the wall heater, changed into some sweats, and knocked on the communicating door. Rosie was in her pajamas. She was clucking over her cowboy boots, soaked to the ankle and damp the rest of the way up.

We settled down on the twin beds, Rosie leaning against the pillows on one, me sitting on the other, and began to talk about what we knew and where we should go from there.

"Let's get to the timetable first," she suggested. I opened my notebook to a clean page.

"First," I said, "came the burglary, or vandalism, or whatever it is. That was Tuesday night, discovered Wednesday morning."

She smiled. "That's the easy part, because we don't know anything much about it."

"Right. Except that it was done sometime during the night and found first thing the next morning. Then it gets complicated." I wrote down "5 P.M. Friday," and circled it. "Starting at about five o'clock this afternoon, right about the time I was leaving the sheriff's office and coming here to meet you. That's when Gracie Piedmont got the call from Spiegel and went out to the spit. It was also right about the time that Perry was telling Clement he'd go out to the spit after he'd gotten some dinner." Rosie had gotten up, taken a few sheets of motel stationery from the desk, plunked herself back on the bed, and begun her own diagram. She's a visual thinker. I guess carpenters tend to be that way.

"What time did we go to the tavern?"

"About six-thirty," I said. "Which is also right about the time that Perry must have found Gracie. Fredda called the cops at six, Perry was radioed at the spit, told to look for Gracie."

"And by seven-thirty the news of her death had somehow gotten to Henry, because that's when he came into the bar to tell Wolf."

"And don't forget Fredda Carey. She made another phone call to the station after seven, and went to the spit." I had scribbled a question mark next to Henry's arrival at the tavern. How had he found out?

"We go to dinner at Nora's. A little later, maybe around eight-fifteen or so, we go out to the spit. Fredda's already there. Wolf has come and gone. The body's been taken away, the coroner's man is out there being futile."

Rosie scribbled for a minute. "That's all pretty tight. Perry says he got to the spit just after six. That means Piedmont died sometime between around five-fifteen—assuming she left her cousin's right at five—and six or six-fifteen."

A question occurred to me. "If Perry was already out there when he got the call, wouldn't he have seen Gracie's car in Spiegel's driveway, wondered where she was, maybe even started looking for her then?"

"He says he didn't. That he hadn't gotten that far out. That he was checking the houses closer in when the call came through."

Remembering Paisley's estimation of Perry's ability, I wondered if he'd been working at all. Still, with what we had, the time of death couldn't be stretched very much beyond the bounds of five-fifteen to six-fifteen.

Moving on to another new notebook page, I said, "People."

Rosie and I have been doing this long enough, now, so the more routine stuff has been reduced to shorthand. She flipped to a clean sheet of stationery.

We started again, with the sperm bank. "Employees," Rosie said. "Especially the one who has a key to the file and tankrooms."

"Doesn't look like the burglar used a key."

"Would you, if everyone knew you had one?"

It was too early in the case for logic, and too late in the evening for it as well. "And the kids, whoever they are, that everyone seems to think did it."

"And the local religious maniacs."

That pretty much took care of that. On to the death. Lots of real people with real names there. Perry. Henry, Wolf's boss and bearer of bad news. Wolf, the boyfriend. Marty Spiegel. Cousin Fredda.

Locations between five and six P.M. Perry, dinner? Henry? We didn't know. Wolf—working at the tavern? We didn't know his hours. Marty Spiegel? He'd gotten the woman out there. Had he really called from L.A.? Fredda? Sitting at Gracie's house, waiting for her to come back? We didn't know.

Our next moves were pretty well laid out for us, then. We would talk to the boyfriend and his boss, and we would see what more we could find out about the dead woman from her cousin. Find out about Spiegel. And, in our spare time, dig out suspects in the break-in.

We turned in, then, wanting to get an early start in the morning. Exhausted as I was from fighting wind and rain and stuffing my head with people and their movements, I had some trouble falling asleep. I lay awake constructing improbable scenarios, rehearsing questions I might ask. Just before I fell asleep I had a shameful thought. Maybe I would get to meet one of the celebrities that lived on the spit.

8

Fredda Carey was in the book, so right before Rosie and I went out for breakfast I called her and asked if we could stop by in an hour or so.

She hesitated.

"My partner and I are trying to put together a piece on this town. The problems, the beauties. The tragedies. You know the kind of thing." I didn't know what kind of thing I was talking about, but I hoped she did. "We want to know about some of the people who live here, and of course about your cousin, who has died so tragically. . . ." *Tragedy* is a word so overused by the media that I figured my overuse of it would be like credentials. Maybe I would remind her of her favorite TV anchorman.

"Oh. Well, I suppose so. But we are bereaved, after all. I hope it won't take too long."

"I'm sure it won't."

Sometime during the night the storm had blown itself inland, where it could batter the Sierras with snow. The morning was fresh and cool, with blue sky and yellow sunlight breaking through little white clouds and bigger gray ones on their way east. I wished them a pleasant journey, brushed the leaves and twigs off the roof and hood of the Chevy, found one tiny scratch, took a deep breath, and thought about food.

Rosie pulled a five-foot-long two-inch-thick eucalyptus branch out of the bed of her truck and volunteered the truck's services for the day.

On the way to Georgia's Café, the place where I'd had my late lunch the day before, we found a shoestore that would probably have boot oil or at least saddle soap for the shoes that had taken such a beating the night before, the ones that were still wet. The shoestore wasn't open yet. We were both wearing sneakers. It was a relief to be carrying something dry and lightweight around on my feet, and I'd been particularly happy to trade the clumsy drapery of the slicker in on a lightweight jacket.

Breakfast was terrific. This time there were more customers, and everyone seemed to be eating the kind of food doctors don't approve of. We both had big fat omelets full of fat calories—mine had cheese and bacon and spinach—and orange juice and strong coffee.

By the time we'd finished, the shoestore had opened, and we bought some leather-saving supplies.

Fredda Carey's house, on a street named Mendocino, was a one-story frame with hardly any paint left on it, an open front porch with a healthy spider plant in a box hooked to the railing, and a weedy front yard supporting a couple of ratty-looking oleanders. Instead of front steps there was a ramp.

The block was midway between downtown and the edge of town, running parallel to and several blocks from the ocean. It was, as a matter of fact, nowhere in particular. Although there were some large trees in some of the yards, none sheltered Fredda Carey's house from the sea wind that had worn it down to bare wood.

Some of the neighboring houses looked better maintained than hers, some showed some landscaping and painting creativity, but there were too many small dirt yards with wire fencing, too many weary old hedges and broken-down cars. Fredda's own ancient station wagon was parked in the drive. Like the house, it didn't have much paint on it.

We walked up the ramp and knocked. The door was opened by a young girl in a wheelchair, which explained the ramp. About twelve, I guessed, but her face was pinched like a worn-out runner's. She wore a big silver cross on a chain around her neck.

"Hello," I said. "We're here to see your mother."

"Yes, I know." I couldn't tell from her voice what she thought of that. "She said to ask you to go on through into the kitchen." She waved a thin hand down the hall toward the back of the house, swung her chair around, and disappeared out the front door. We walked down the hall.

The kitchen was big, like kitchens in old houses are, unless someone's ruined the old house. The painted cabinets looked like the originals, but the stove and the refrigerator and the big freezer in the corner looked new.

Fredda Carey was rolling out a ball of dough on a big floured wooden board on the kitchen table. A nice, homey scene. The night before she had been wrapped in plastic against the weather, and about all I'd noticed about her was that she was a big woman with a fretful face. I got a better look at her now. She was tall and broad, but not fat, with wide shoulders. A square face with prominent cheekbones, her brown hair hanging straight to just below her shoulders. Her brown eyes had heavy lids smudged with brown eye shadow. Her hands, wrapped tightly around the roller handles, were big enough to go with the rest of her, with square-tipped fingers and chipped polish on the short nails. She was one of those women who should wear men's shirts—the cheap, frilly blue blouse was too tight across the shoulders. Her old faded big-bottom bells nearly covered the blue sneakers worn thin over the big toes. Her face still looked fretful.

She invited us to sit down at the table and talk while she worked. It was a nice old table, scrubbed pine, but the chairs were plastic and chrome and ugly. There were two sheets of baked cookies on top of the refrigerator and a big pile of plastic freezer bags on the counter nearby. I started to say something, but she peered at her watch and turned away, taking down the two cookie sheets, grabbing a handful of plastic bags, dumping cookies into the bags. She put the bags on a large metal tray, carried the tray to the upright freezer, and stashed the cookies inside, where there must have been a thousand cookies in plastic bags already stored.

She finished making cutouts in the dough she'd just rolled, put the cutouts on the two liberated cookie sheets, opened the oven, took out two sheets of baked cookies, put those on the refrigerator, and loaded the oven with the new batch. Then she looked at her watch again, pulled another large dough ball out of an immense mixing bowl, and plopped it down on the wooden board.

"I bet you think that's a lot of cookies for one woman and one little girl," she said slyly, pointing at the freezer. I said yes, it certainly seemed to be. "It's my business. I sell them to the grocery, the restaurants. Especially in summer, when more business comes through. This year I'm expanding. Got a customer up in Rosewood, north of here. Fredda's sugar cookies. All natural."

We told her we thought that was terrific, which pleased her.

"Now," she said, whacking the doughball with her rolling pin, "what can I help you with?"

"Wait a second," I said, scribbling in my notebook. "Fredda's all natural cookies. That's Fredda with two D's?"

"Yes. Two." She began mashing the dough flat. I finished writing with a flourish.

"They smell very good," Rosie said politely.

"Oh, gee. I bet you'd like some. And some coffee." She scraped a half dozen off the sheets on the refrigerator and onto a plastic plate, set the plate and two cups down in front of us, turned on the flame under a percolator, checked her watch again, and went back to rolling dough.

"About the town," Rosie began. "Have you lived here all your life?" Fredda nodded. The dough was nearly subjugated. "And your cousin?"

She sighed, set down her rolling pin, and went to the stove for the percolator of warmed-over coffee. She poured some into our cups and seemed to assume we both drank it black.

"She lived here all her life too."

"I guess most of the people in town are people you grew up with?" I asked.

"A lot of them, anyway."

"Like Wolf, over at the tavern?"

She nodded, picked one of the cookies off the plate, took a bite, then another, then one more and it was gone. Back to the dough. Another forearm-bulging roll and it was a quarter inch thick. "And Nora, at the sperm bank?"

"That's right. Of course, Nora was a little older than me,

so we weren't close as kids or anything. Wolf's more like my age. Poor Wolf." She shook her head. "I guess he's all broken up about this."

"You guess?" Rosie said.

"Well, I'm sure he is."

I wanted to know more about Wolf, but at the moment I was more interested in the bank. "How do you feel about—how do people in town feel about—the sperm bank?"

She ate another cookie. "The sperm bank? I don't know. You got to give Nora a lot of credit. She's a smart one. I was kind of surprised when she came back here, but I can't say I blame her. It's exciting down in the city, but personally, I wouldn't want to live there. Too expensive."

"And, of course," Rosie added, "there's more crime."

"That's for sure." She stamped out a new bunch of circles, looked at her watch, went to the oven, took out the two sheets, set them on top of the stove while she emptied the two that had been cooling into freezer bags, and finished up the routine by sliding the new ones into the oven and checking her watch yet again. Then she took the dough left over from the two previous cuttings, rolled it in with the dough in the bowl, and dropped another wad onto the board.

"How do you feel about the crime that happened at the bank?" Rosie persisted.

Fredda shrugged. "Same way everyone else in town feels. Kids. Probably that Rollie and Tommy Hackman. Real leaders, those two, real funny boys."

"Are they bad kids? Get in trouble a lot?"

She backed off a little. "Oh, well, you know what I mean. High-spirited. I can see how they might think that was just about the funniest thing ever, ripping off a bunch of . . . but they're not mean boys. They never tease Joanne or anything."

"Joanne?"

"My daughter."

"These Hackman boys—they're brothers?" I asked, sipping some of the bitter coffee.

"Yeah. Live right down the street. Just a few doors." She paused, cocked her head, looked at the back door, and stood up and headed toward it. At that instant there was the sound of a key turning in the lock. The door opened and Joanne wheeled into the kitchen.

"We're talking," Fredda said. "Take a cookie and go to your room." The child started to do half of what she was told—she didn't take a cookie—but Fredda stopped her. "Wait a minute. Where's the key? You put it right back under the pot, where it belongs." Joanne sighed and returned to the back porch, replacing the key under a flowerpot. Then she spun the chair, slammed the back door, and we heard her wheelchair roll away.

"Kid's locked me out more than once, palming that key," Fredda complained.

I took a cookie off the plate and bit into it. No nuts, no raisins, no chips, not much taste beyond sweet. Dry and dusty. I put it on the table next to my coffee cup. "Do you mind talking about your cousin? I know it just happened and everything . . ."

She shrugged again. "Oh, that's okay. It's painful, but maybe it's better to talk." She sat down, the lump of dough untouched on the board, the rolling pin beside it.

"Then about this accident last night, could you go over that once more? Why she went? When?"

"It's like I told Clement. And Perry. She went out to see if everything was okay with Marty's house. He called her. Asked her about it. Around five it was. We were talking. We'd just had a glass of wine. She was going to fry some fish for us."

"How much wine had she had, do you think?"

Fredda ate another cookie. "Just the one glass, I seem to remember. But, you know, I'm not really sure. She could have had a whole other bottle before I came. How would I know?"

"What time did you get there?"

"Must have been a little after four-thirty."

"You think she was drunk?" Rosie asked.

"Not so I could see."

"Did she usually drink a lot?"

"No. All I'm saying is how would I know what she did before I was even there?"

"So," I said, "Marty called around five. They were pretty close?"

"Close?" She got up, poured herself an inch of coffee, and sat back down again. "I wouldn't say close. I don't think he was really close to anyone in town. Kind of full of himself, if you ask me. Maybe a little snobbish, if you know what I mean. No, see, Gracie was a movie freak. You know, she knew all about Cary Grant and Veronica Lake and people like that. All the old ones. And I guess they got started talking once. Had something in common. Friends, that way. If he ever talked to anyone else, it would have been different, but he didn't, so she was the one he called."

She made it sound like the woman had died because she liked old movies.

I ate the rest of my cookie so she wouldn't be insulted. "Where was he calling from?"

"L.A."

"And you and your daughter were there when he called?"

"Not Joanne. I took Joanne over to her great-aunt's place. She likes it there." A grimace.

"You don't?" I asked.

"Oh, she's okay. My mother's sister. It's just that she's all the time talking about Jesus this, Jesus that. Joanne's kind of gotten into it too." She shrugged, a by-now familiar gesture that she seemed to use as a good-natured expression of "what the hell." She looked at her watch, said "Whoops," and went to the oven. Another batch of cookies, a bit on the brown side. She repeated her procedure up to the point of putting another batch in the oven. She didn't have any ready.

"I'm getting behind in the system, here." She frowned. "I forgot to roll out some more to go in when those came out." She floured the board again, dropped another ball of dough on it, and began to smash away.

"We won't keep you much longer," I told her. "So she got this phone call and took off?"

"That's right." The dough didn't have a chance. In a couple of minutes it looked like a steamroller had gotten it. "She said she'd just run over for a minute. It got longer and longer and I was sitting there getting worried, so I finally called Clement."

Rosie, who is usually very polite, had not finished her cookie. She asked, "What were you afraid might have happened?"

"Oh, listen, in that storm? Anything. A tree could have fell on her car. Somebody's roof could come off and land on her head. Anything."

"And you called back . . ." I prodded.

"Yeah, well, it was after seven and I still hadn't heard anything. So finally I called the cops again. Angie told me they'd found her body. That was when I drove out to see." She shook her head. "I saw, all right. I couldn't believe it, you know? They were hauling her dead body up with ropes." She wiped her eyes.

Rosie and I had been lucky, I thought. We'd gotten there when the body was already gone. I like it better that way.

"Did you identify her?"

"Heck, no. Clement did. You think I wanted to go out there and look at her?"

"Of course not," Rosie commiserated. "And then Wolf showed up, too, right?" Fredda nodded. "He seems like a real sweet guy. We were in the tavern when he got the news. It knocked him right over."

"Oh, sure. He's the best. They seemed to get along pretty good too. They were probably going to get married." She was cutting out circles of dough again.

"Henry mentioned that Wolf's had a lot of problems," I said. "Is that so?"

"Oh, nothing too big. Women. He had a marriage that didn't work out. There was a kid too. And before that he had a thing for Nora, that was when they were pretty young. And she dumped him and took off for the city. Said she had things to do. Well, she did them and came back, but by then it was too late. Not that she came back for him. I heard she got homesick. Wanted to have a more, you know, natural life. By the way, be sure and put in that write-up that these cookies are all natural. No artificial ingredients."

I thought it was probably time to go. She was putting two more cookie sheets into the oven. I don't like to wear out my sources in one sitting, and besides, I was getting dizzy watching her.

We thanked her, assured her we didn't need to be escorted to the door, and walked back down the hallway. Joanne was sitting on the front porch. "Is that your truck, with the dog in it?" Rosie said it was. "You going to write about my mother?"

"Maybe," I answered, feeling guilty. "I'll bet you're glad your mom is in the cookie business, right? You get to eat all those cookies."

She laughed, a short bark. "So what? She gave you some, didn't she?" I said yes, she had. "They're not very good, are they?" She swung her chair around and rolled to the other end of the porch, dismissing us.

We returned to Georgia's Café for some non-Fredda coffee. I hadn't noticed them before, but there they were, in a cardboard box on the counter: plastic bags with gummed mailing labels on them that said "Fredda's All-Natural Cookies." The label was hand-lettered neatly in ballpoint.

I was thinking I'd like to talk to Nora again, maybe get some background on Wolf and her relationship with him. Rosie mentioned she thought we ought to talk to the Hackman boys. Maybe we'd find out, after all, that the break-in had been an adolescent joke. In which case, she said sadly, Gracie Piedmont's death was probably just an accident and there was no case of any kind. She was depressing me to the point of agreeing with her. Which turned her around.

"No," she said. "I don't really believe any of that."

I noticed that Fredda's cookies were also on the menu, under Desserts. Fifty cents apiece. "You don't want to go home yet."

She laughed. "You're right. I want there to be a case, and as long as she's dead anyway, she may just as well have been murdered."

Nora didn't answer her home phone, so we went over to the bank. The receptionist was there and sent us up after consulting with her intercom. But when we got to Nora's door, which was ajar, we heard two voices. I knocked.

"Just a second," she called out. "See you later, then, Marty?"

A short, muscular man wearing thick glasses brushed out past us, with just the quickest nod in our direction. I turned to watch him go before entering the office. He looked familiar.

"Marty?" I asked. She nodded. "Spiegel?" Yes, she admitted, it was.

Rosie was impressed, but she tended to business. "I guess he flew up here because he never got a return call from Gracie Piedmont last night? To check on his house?"

"I suppose so," Nora said.

"And you're buddies?" I asked. "He just dropped in to say hi?"

"Don't be silly." She played with a stack of papers on her desk. "He was here on business."

"Business? What kind of business? Bank business?"

She didn't answer me. "What did you need to see me about, anyway?"

"Look, if you want us to investigate, you're going to have to give us information freely." Actually, I was curious as hell.

"All right. But this is highly confidential. We always keep this information very strictly to ourselves."

It turned out that the famous Marty Spiegel was what the guy in the bar had called a "depositor."

I filed that information under "fascinating but irrelevant" and turned to Nora's private life.

— **9** —

Nora had, it turned out, been very heavily involved with Wolf Oswald, but that had been a very long time ago. They had dated sporadically in high school, more seriously when she was attending junior college. He had wanted to get married. She had taken a series of jobs in the county, "nothing very exciting," and had put him off while she tried to decide what she wanted to do.

What she wanted to do, after all, was leave, go to San Francisco, and work in the financial district at whatever she could find. She had worked, and she had learned. She had gone to school at night and taken business courses. There had been occasional weekends in Wheeler for a while, but finally he had married someone else, and he and Nora became, she said, friends. That marriage had fizzled a couple of years before she had come back to Wheeler to stay.

I was beginning to understand what Fredda had meant about Wolf's problems with women, but his story didn't seem very different from anyone else's. Not very different, for example, from mine. A lot of us had limped footloose in one way or another through the seventies. Periods of realignment are hard on everyone, especially when they end up with absolutely nothing having been changed by all that agony.

"When you came back to town," Rosie asked, "what happened between you then? He was free, wasn't he?"

"He was free, but nothing happened. We went out once or twice, but it didn't work."

Rosie persisted. "And he never resented you for not marrying him?"

"I think he was relieved, when he got to know me again later. Relieved that we hadn't gotten married. I'm not the easiest person to get along with and I love to work. I don't think that's the kind of wife he had in mind." She sighed. "Poor Gracie. She would have been right for him. Poor Wolf. Anyway"—she drummed her fingers on her desk—"I really don't think any of this has any significance. It's all years and years ago."

"You say Gracie would have been perfect for him," I said. "How?" All she had ever said about Gracie before was that she was a good employee and was "sweet," whatever that means.

"Oh, you know. Feminine in a traditional way. She would have let him take the lead, make the decisions. She wasn't assertive at all as far as I could tell. Don't misunderstand—I liked her."

"But you weren't friends," Rosie said.

The phone rang. She picked it up, asked the party on the other end to hold on, covered the mouthpiece, and said, "Listen, guys, I've got an appointment in five minutes. Could we pick this up again later?"

We said good-bye.

I was thinking about those "years and years" since she and Wolf had been together. It didn't mean much. A man can carry a heartache around for decades. A relationship that should have worked and didn't—because you were too young and stupid, maybe—can leave you looking for that person for the rest of your life. I had one like that. It has been years and years, and a lot of women, including one marriage, in between. And if I knew where she was, I'd go and get her. If she was still the person I remembered.

It was early. I figured we should go look for Marty Spiegel, Gracie's friend, and that the place to look for him was probably the house he'd been so worried about.

The road out along the spit was still slick with mud now half-dried. A birch tree had fallen onto the road, but it was passable. The big trees sheltering the houses didn't look much the worse for wear, all in all, but there were branches scattered on the road and in what we could see of the yards.

In daylight, without blinding wind and rain, the spit was a beautiful place. The ocean was as quiet as it ever gets up here, and the air was fresh and salty. The glimpses of wealth between the trees didn't spoil the effect one bit, although, on the way out to Marty's, I noticed a couple of houses that didn't look so great. One was modest. One was even humble, with plywood still covering the windows from the night before.

We stopped at the bottom of the driveway where, the night before, Gracie's car had been parked. In its place now was an old red Jaguar. We didn't doubt for a second that we'd found the right driveway. The Jaguar's license plate said MOVIES. We left Alice sleeping in the car and walked up to the door.

It was quite a door.

One of those big double jobs, about ten feet tall, but not the kind you'd expect a butler to answer. Eric the Red, maybe, but not a butler. It was made of thick rough redwood slabs with monstrous black iron strap hinges. The small round windows on either side of the door were heavy leaded glass pictures of sailing vessels of some ancient and indeterminate origin.

The house went nicely with the doors. Very big. This was no rustic crackerbox covered with plywood siding and batten board. The front exterior was solid, with no windows other than the little leaded jobs by the door, and made of thick redwood planking set on the diagonal. I looked up. There was some transparent glass on what could have been the second or third floor, depending on the downstairs ceilings, but it was screened on the inside with potted plants. At least I supposed they were potted.

All he needed was a moat. I couldn't wait to see the inside. I grabbed the big iron ring that hung from the door, but Rosie poked my arm and, reaching alongside the doorframe, pressed an electric bell. We heard it resound deep inside the building, a throaty two-note chime. A window slammed up somewhere around the side of the house and a voice yelled, "Who is it?"

"Friends of Nora Canfield," I yelled back. "We need to talk to you."

Sometime later, maybe two minutes, a small door set in one half of the big doors swung back. Spiegel was frowning, his chunky shoulders cast aggressively forward. He was dressed in a T-shirt and those little shorts people run in. The T-shirt didn't say anything. I noticed the heavy glasses were held together on one side with a small safety pin.

"What's the problem?" he wanted to know.

"No problem," I said, and was about to launch into my *Probe* magazine scam when I realized the spiel wouldn't work with him. He'd dealt with the press too often, and I thought I remembered something about how hard it was for reporters to get to see him. So I played it straight.

"We're looking into some things for Nora, and we want to talk to you about the accident out here last night."

"Accident?" He slumped against the doorjamb, the aggressive stance suddenly gone. "You mean Gracie. You some kind of private cops?"

I shrugged and nodded, a half statement he could interpret any way he wanted. "Actually, we were looking into the break-in at the bank, but then this happened. This accident . . ." Again, I let him fill in the blanks. "Could we come in and talk to you about it?"

He tightened up again, and danced a couple of steps in place, like he was going to start sparring. "I'm kind of busy. There was some damage to the house. I haven't even checked every room yet."

"We won't take much of your time," Rosie said.

"Well, okay. But I don't know much about last night. I was in L.A. I feel so bad that she came out here—can you understand that I'm not feeling too great about that? Shit. Come on in, then, for a few minutes. I'm not trying to be hostile or inhospitable or anything, you know, it's just that a lot of people are always bothering me. . . . Come on in." Finally, he stood aside and we entered.

The man was in great shape. Short, maybe five foot seven, but every inch was pared down to the muscle. I'd been doing some bicycling lately, and my spare tire was nearly gone. But he made me feel flabby. I resented it.

The entry hall was big and square and empty except for several black iron coat hooks screwed into the paneled wall. The floor was quarry tile. He led us across the tile into an immense room that would have done service as a Saxon Great Hall. Squares of white plaster wall were framed in chunky redwood. The vaulted ceiling was crossed by beams a foot wide and two feet deep. The floor was pegged hardwood planking. Along one wall was a stone fireplace with a firebox that must have been five feet across. Along the back of the room were anachronistic sliding glass doors leading to a deck. There wasn't a lot of furniture, just a seating arrangement, facing the fireplace, consisting of an eight-foot brown leather couch, a couple of leather chairs, and a few obviously hand-hewn tables. The rug on which the furniture sat also looked handmade, Scandinavian, and very thick. A wide staircase led up to a gallery, along the front of the house, above the entry hall, with a row of windows filled with plants in big pots—the ones I'd seen from outside—and to doors on either side that I guessed led to second-floor rooms.

I don't enter the homes of strangers with any expectations, or at least I try not to. But once invited in, I do tend to halfway expect to be asked to sit down. It didn't happen.

"Just on my way to take a look at the pool when the bell rang," he said. "Come on."

He trotted toward the back of the living room and made a sharp left through a swinging door into a smaller room, only twenty by twenty. It was a well-equipped gym, with the same hardwood floor as the living room but no fancy beams. Just white plaster walls and surgical chrome. A rowing machine, a treadmill, an exercise cycle, a slant board, and one of those multi-station weight machines. The back wall, like the one in the living room, was glass. One section was broken, with a large branch poking through and rainwater on the floor. Outside the glass I could see more deck and a big covered swimming pool. The cover, and the deck, were littered with debris from the trees.

"Take a seat somewhere," he said, waving at the exercise equipment. Then he slid back a glass door and went outside. The weight equipment offered a couple of seats, so we sat, watching him poke around.

"He's rich," I said to Rosie. "He can be as weird as he wants to be."

"And creative. Don't forget creative."

He returned quickly. He seemed to do everything quickly.

"Pool looks okay. Hot tub's okay. Lost some roof tiles," he reported as though we might actually care. "Be right with you." He disappeared through a thick doorway with a tiny window in it. Rosie gave me a look, and I grinned back at her. He popped out again. "Sauna's fine. No leaks."

He arranged himself on the rowing machine, taking off his glasses, placing them carefully on the floor, and setting a timer. "Do you mind if I do a few things while we talk?" He didn't wait for an answer, but began pulling. "I missed my workout this morning, flying up here." Before either of us could speak, he added, "Tell me what it's like being a P.I."

"A lot of the time," Rosie said, "it's pretty tedious."

"Bet it's fun. Admit that it's fun. What does it take to get a license?"

"I don't know," I admitted. "I don't have one."

He laughed. Pull. Pull. Pull. "I guess you don't want to talk about it, am I right? Okay, ask away."

"You don't seem very upset about Gracie's death," I said.

He looked as though he considered stopping his rhythmic chore, thought better of it, and kept on going. "Of course I'm upset. I feel shitty. I told you. But I'm not devastated. She was a nice person, and we liked talking to each other. But nothing really close. I feel guilt more than loss."

Nicely put, I thought. He was creative, all right.

"There's something I don't quite get, though," Rosie said. "All she had to do was come out here, walk around the house, take a look, and go home again. But she didn't do that. She went and stood out on the scarp to watch the waves coming in to get her. Why would she do a thing like that?"

"Wouldn't you? It must have been magnificent out here last night."

"I don't know," Rosie said. "I doubt it. The question is, would *she*?"

He thought about it, rowing that damned machine to nowhere. "Are you saying maybe she didn't? That something else happened?"

"I doubt it," I said. "But on the off chance that the death is related to the break-in at the sperm bank, we're just checking out possibilities. Eliminating the extraneous if we can."

He raised his eyebrows, turning to look at me, just as his timer went off.

"I don't know what she'd do. She had to have had a romantic streak—she loved those old movies—but I guess I never thought of her as a person who took chances. I never really thought about it one way or the other. But you never can tell about people. Maybe she was feeling reckless. Maybe she'd had a fight with her boyfriend or something and was playing out some dramatic scenario." He stood up, shook himself, and trotted over to the treadmill. He set it at a good jog and took off.

"Did they fight much?" I asked. "Gracie and Wolf?"

He shook his head. "We never talked about things like that. Except once she did say, jokingly, that he seemed to be a little jealous of our friendship."

"And you're sure there was nothing to be jealous of? Maybe on her side?"

He was sweating and breathing hard, finally. "I never noticed anything emotional."

"So you called from L.A.," Rosie said. He nodded, sweat dripping off his chin. "Why did you call her instead of the local police?"

"I never thought of the police. I just called to ask her about the storm, and she offered to check the house. That seemed okay. When I hadn't heard from her by this morning, I decided to come up. And Clement told me about her accident."

Rosie continued. "Was anyone with you when you called?"

He shook his head, laughing. "You're serious about this, aren't you? I really was in L.A. I've got a plane ticket somewhere around from this morning."

"Is that the only reason you came up? To check on the house?" Rosie asked.

He glanced sideways at her. Was he blushing or just turning red from exertion? I would have been turning red from exertion.

"What do you mean?" he asked.

"Well," I eased into it, "there was that theft at the sperm bank. And we saw you there this morning."

He turned off the treadmill, hopped off, and trotted over to the cycle. I didn't push for an answer. He got on the cycle and started pedaling.

"We're investigating what happened over there—that's why we came to Wheeler in the first place. And I guess I was wondering if you had any ideas about why it might have happened. The break-in."

He was breathing harder, blowing noisily like jocks do when they're pushing it.

"I heard it was religious nuts. Nora said there was a note."

"Could be," I said. "I guess there'll be a lot of activity around there for a while until they restock."

"Yeah." His dark curly hair was soaked with sweat.

"I've always been kind of curious about why a man would do that. What his motive might be. To have his sperm frozen that way. To be sold to a stranger."

"Don't know. Lots of different reasons for doing it, lots of situations. Ask Nora."

Since I already had, I moved on to other things. "Do you know Fredda Carey?"

"Fredda? Gracie's cousin? We've met." He was grunting with every breath, but he kept going. Rosie must have gotten tired watching him, because she was lying down on the slant board.

"Were she and Gracie close? They were having dinner that night."

He got off the cycle, went to a shelf in the corner and grabbed a big white towel. He wiped the sweat off his chest, arms, and hands. "They saw each other once in a while, I guess. They seemed like pretty different types, but they got along like relatives do, as far as I could tell." He asked me to vacate the bench, tossed the towel on the floor, and lay down. I stood, watching him pump iron.

"How were they different?"

"Gracie was nicer. I mean, I don't know Fredda, really, but the couple of times we met it seemed to me she was kind of pissed off at life or something. Always trying to cut a deal. Gracie said it had to do with her kid being born crippled. I don't know."

"Where's Fredda's husband?" Rosie wanted to know. She was still lying on the slant board.

"Never heard there was one."

"You going to be around for a few days?" I asked.

"Yeah." Grunt. "Got some repairs to see to. I need some time off, anyway." He swung his feet to the floor and sat there, looking up at me. Rosie got off the slant board and stood next to me. "I'd like to hear more about the work you guys do," he said.

Sure, I told him, maybe we could have a beer or something. I wanted to hear more about what he did too. Rich people can be pretty interesting, and I almost liked this one.

He showed us out. I said we'd be in touch. He was wearing his thick glasses again, and his eyes looked tiny.

—*10*—

Clement was sitting at his desk, staring at some paperwork. He looked happy to see us.

"I was just trying to think of an excuse to make another pot of coffee. Want some?"

I didn't, really, but said I did. Rosie asked for some water for Alice, who was sitting outside the door.

"Bring her in. I got a soup bowl around here somewhere."

Once we were all set up with liquid refreshment, I got to the point of our visit.

"Anything on Gracie Piedmont?"

"Only that she didn't drown. No water in her lungs."

"What did she die of?" Rosie asked.

"Her head was crushed in. But then, the rest of her was banged up too. Those rocks are pretty bad."

"Any way to tell if all the damage was done by rocks?" I doubted it, but I had to ask.

He shook his head. "Let's just say there wasn't any damage that couldn't have been done by rocks."

"What about the car?"

"Nothing yet."

"What do you think?" I persisted.

He shook his head again. "She was washed clean, jammed stuck down there on the rocks with the water washing her. Hard to tell if one wound killed her and the rest of them didn't bleed. Hard to tell anything. You got any reasons to suppose someone did this to her somehow?"

It was my turn to shake my head. "None."

Angie walked in the door, said hello to us, asked if we had enough coffee, and, reassured, moved on into the back room.

"Well." Clement took a last slug of coffee and sighed deeply. "I got a bunch of little stuff to deal with here." He tapped his finger on the pile of papers.

"I wanted to ask you," I said. "How did Henry find out about Gracie?"

"I told him," Angie chirped from the other room.

"One more thing," I said. "We want to have a look at the spot where the sperm was dumped. Can you tell us where it is?"

"Sure. You won't see much down there, though. What you do is, you take Cellini to the coast road, and on past the Spicer Street access . . ." He caught our blank looks, laughed, and picked up a ballpoint. He scribbled some lines, blobs, and words on a sheet of notepaper and slid it across the desk. "You're here," he said, pointing at a cross labeled "downtown," at the far left of the sketchy map. "Cellini's the next street over here, crosses Main. Runs into the coast road, here. You turn right onto the road and go north. About half a mile on you pass where Spicer comes in. All along in there you're pretty high up above the beach. You go a little farther then, and you'll see a kind of dip between the dunes. Big path down to the beach there. That's the spot." He pointed to some blobs he'd drawn out beyond the line of the beach. "Rocks out there make a kind of triangle formation close in. That's where the stuff was, what we found of it. Tangled up in the seaweed around those rocks." Over at the far right of the map he'd shown the spit, another half-mile or so beyond the triangle rocks. The coast road crossed the road out onto the spit, the one we'd taken on our way out from Nora's hillside home, east of town, the night before.

"You going to keep on looking into Gracie's death?"

"I think so," I answered.

"I'm not saying you're wrong. I just don't have anything to go on. Maybe if I had better help. Or if I had anything to convince the sheriff with, so I could get some help from them. But the county plays straight poker, and you're look- ing at one hell of a lot of wild cards, with the break-in and the death."

"You play poker, Clement?" Rosie asked.

"Sure do. Don't always have time, but I like to get a game going once in a while. You?"

"Once in a while. But Jake does it every week."

"If I can," I said.

Clement looked pleased. "Maybe we ought to get a game going tonight at my place. Perry plays. He plays stupid, but that's okay with me."

"Should we see if we can round up a couple more people?" Rosie asked.

"You bet." He took the map back from me, and added another blob—the location and address of his house.

"Oh, by the way, Clement," I said. "The Hackman boys. Are they the ones you think might be responsible for the break-in?"

"Who told you that, for Christ's sake?" He frowned. "Well, could be. It was Rollie hanging around the beach the morning we found the stuff, but he hangs around there all the time, anyway. Hell, sometimes kids get in trouble. . . . And in a way, if he did it, maybe he would want to watch and see what happened next. Or maybe he'd want to be as far away . . . I don't know, forget I said anything."

We thanked him for the information he'd given us, and walked down the street to the tavern. It was noon, and Wolf had just unlocked the doors. He looked haggard and he moved slowly.

We ordered mineral water. He handed us the bottles and glasses of ice with twists of lime. "I hear you two have been asking a lot of questions about Gracie's accident."

"Where'd you hear that?" Rosie asked. He didn't answer her.

"I hear you're some kind of writers or reporters."

I nodded. "Where'd you hear that?" I asked.

"From just about everybody. What are you here to report, anyway?"

I gave him the song and dance about writing a piece on the town, small town with sperm bank. "And, of course," I added, "a death . . . well, it just seems to be part of kind of thing that's been happening around here lately."

"You mean like a bad-luck town or something?"

"I guess."

"Sounds a little peculiar to me. Some of the people in town aren't so sure they believe that. Henry thinks you're private investigators."

Rosie broke in. "Investigators? Why wouldn't we admit that? Besides, reporters work in teams. Investigators don't."

Sometimes I marvel at Rosie's ability to make bald statements of fact about things she knows nothing about. A real and useful talent.

"That makes sense," he said, and began washing glasses. The glasses, I reflected, must have been left from the night before, because we'd opened the place and there was no one there but us. The glasses looked clean to start with, though, so I decided it was just busy work.

"I didn't expect to see you in here today," I said. "Pretty upsetting for you, about Gracie."

A muscle in his cheek twitched. He kept washing clean glasses. "Better to keep working."

"You two were planning on getting married, right?" Rosie asked.

"Right." He didn't look up.

No reason to beat around the bush, I thought. "Do you think it was an accident?" He did look up, then, straight at me. His eyes were bloodshot.

"What the hell are you after?"

I kept on going. "Do you think she would have gone out on the edge to look at the waves? She was just there to check one of the houses."

He stared at me. "Don't try to make a big story out of this, pal. She fell. Leave her alone."

Rosie took a turn. "You don't know of anyone who might have wanted to hurt her?"

He glared back at her. "I bet you'd just love it if I pushed her. Just like a man, right?" He shoved our two dollars back at us, and spoke to me. "Drinks are on the house. There's nobody who would have wanted to hurt Gracie, and don't try to say there was. Now, get out of here. I don't want to talk. I don't want to talk to you."

I decided this was not a good time to invite him to a poker game, not a good day to get to know him better. We left.

We stopped for a quick lunch at a place we hadn't tried before. It was called the Santa Rosa Plum, and the menu in the window had a lot of sprout and avocado kinds of things. Our waitress was a tired-looking woman who was polite but morose. We were just deciding to make the beach our next stop when she dragged herself over to take our order. We both ordered the vegetarian sandwiches—cheese, avocado, sprouts, and tomato on whole wheat. The waitress nodded to someone in the booth behind us, and said, "Be right with you, Henry."

Henry it was, finishing his coffee and waiting for his check. He smiled at us. We smiled back. He got his check and left.

We had just made the first dents in our sandwiches when Fredda came in the door, carrying a cardboard carton. Our waitress went to talk to her. Most of it looked like chat, except when Fredda started stacking bags of cookies next to the cash register. Our waitress stopped her after the first dozen. They had a mild discussion. Fredda shrugged, turned, waved at us, and left carrying her carton, still nearly full.

After lunch we headed back to the truck, which was parked outside Clement's office. Just as we passed the grocery store, the Jaguar with the MOVIES license plate pulled up.

Spiegel, dressed in rustic denim and plaid flannel, jumped out and greeted us in a friendly fashion.

"Where you headed?"

"Couple places. Beach, for one. Glad we ran into you," I said. "We're getting up a poker game for tonight over at Clement's. Interested?"

He looked slightly suspicious. "What kind of stakes are you talking about?"

"Nickel ante."

He thought about it. "What time?"

"I guess around eight."

"Who's playing?"

I reflected that celebrity must be hard on this man some-times. "Rosie and Clement, me, Perry. Maybe give Nora a call."

"Maybe so. It'd be a relief to do something besides think about work."

I wrote down Paisley's address for him, he went into the grocery store, and we continued on our way to the truck. After stopping for gas, we headed for the beach.

— *11*—

We took Cellini Avenue, which sloped downward through the center of town and ended a few feet above sea level at the coast road.

Sand, driftwood, even seaweed had forced itself through the bottleneck formed by the beach entrance path cut across the dunes. The storm's debris was scattered across the sur-face of the road itself and made the right turn an obstacle course which Rosie negotiated skillfully.

We followed the narrow road north. It wound along the edge of town, rising gradually above the beach until, at Spicer, I could see only the shoulder of the road and the ocean some distance below. Another half mile and we spot-ted the entrance Clement had marked on his map. Rosie made a U-turn, pulling the truck up onto the shoulder just beyond the path.

We stood on the rise for a moment, looking down at the beach, a cup deep enough, here, to contain its own evidence of the gale.

The triangular rock formation, at low tide, was near the edge of the beach. We picked our way out through weed and wood and, here and there, the corpse of a fish or bird caught by the storm. There were bits of glass in the sand, bits of plastic, shell, unidentifiable objects. I squinted at the rocks and tried to see someone, anyone, tossing vials of sperm for the rocks to catch like sea lions catching fish. I kept getting confused between vials of sperm caught on the rocks and a woman's body that had been caught by different rocks on a different part of the beach. Alice was prancing at the edge of the water, playing tag with the gentle waves. Rosie stood, arms akimbo, looking toward the spit, which was clearly visible to the north. I tossed a stick for the dog a few times, feeling futile. There was nothing here to find because there was too much of everything. We began to walk toward the spit.

We'd gone about two-thirds of the way, when I saw something pink fluttering slowly down the side of the spit and onto the beach. Gradually, as it came closer, it took shape. A woman, dressed in some kind of pink pajamas.

Alice ran to meet her, and I heard her laugh as she stooped to pet the dog. A nice sound.

She was somewhere around forty-five. Slightly thick in the waist, with graying long auburn hair and nearly black eyes. She smiled at us. It was a very sexy smile. For whom, I wondered.

We said hello. She said hello. She stopped. "I'll bet you're those reporters everyone's been talking about. Or are you detectives? Which are you, anyway?"

We introduced ourselves. "Reporters," I said. "*Probe* magazine."

"That's very exciting." The smile was definitely for me. "I'm Melody Clift. I have a house up there." She waved an arm toward the spit.

"The writer!" Rosie exclaimed as if she were a fan.

Melody Clift ducked her head modestly. I'd never read one of her romances and I didn't think I ever would, but I looked at her with new interest. The pink pajamas were a mite flashy, but you couldn't tell from her manner or her soft voice that she'd made several million dollars writing porn for women.

She smiled a conspiratorial smile. "Yes, I do write. And I'm dying to know what kind of dirt you're digging up about this town."

"Maybe something you can use?" I smiled.

She laughed. "Why not?" She took my arm, which I found somewhat startling. But then, she was a startling woman. "Why don't you drop in on me later and we can talk." Although she smiled at Rosie, I wasn't sure the invitation was for both of us. "My house is the seventh one out."

I told her we would try, but might not make it that day.

"I'll be in all evening, and all day tomorrow. Please drop by. I'm feeling very bored. It can be so dismal here in the winter." There was an edge of mysterious sadness in her soft, husky voice. The day was bright and sunny and far from dismal.

"I guess you came up this morning?" Rosie asked. "To take a look at your house?"

"Yes. From my home in San Francisco."

"Is everything all right?"

"I'm afraid there's a tree in my swimming pool."

We "tsked" in sympathy. "We should be going now," I said. All that soft pinkness was making me nervous.

"I hope I'll see you later, then. You, too, Rosie. And of course the poodle. She's lovely."

We said good-bye. She walked on down the beach and we continued toward the spit.

Rosie was chuckling. "She likes you, Jake. I could feel the steam rising."

"Oh, come on."

"Really. If I were Lee, I'd be worried about you visiting that woman." I snorted. Lee is someone I've been seeing, off and on, for several months. A bright, beautiful attorney. She lives in Petaluma, which is nearly an hour away from Oakland. She works long hours and rarely makes the commute, which leaves it up to me. I'd been managing it a couple of times a week. She doesn't think that's enough, and accuses me of taking the relationship lightly. She is unjust.

"I think," I said, "that we should visit Melody anyway. She might know something."

Rosie laughed. "I'll bet she knows a lot." I grunted. "I think you should go to see her alone. I think she'd talk more freely, if she has anything to talk about."

I grunted again. "Have you actually read her books?"

"No."

"Sure?"

"Positive."

We had reached the path that Melody had taken down to the beach from the spit above, a rocky, steep, ankle-twister zigzagging down the cleft where the spit joined the mainland. Not posted as private, spit-dweller property, but somehow seeming that way. Farther out toward the water, the scarp was nearly vertical, with a slight overhang, clay and rock crumbling to sand halfway down. Out still farther, midway along the spit, were the clusters of rock, broken and sharp, tumbled together like jagged eggs in a nest of foam, where Gracie Piedmont had fallen.

It looked to me like she could have gotten as good a view of the stormy ocean from a softer, more inland part of the spit, if that's what she wanted to do, like the part over the beach. I said as much to Rosie.

"But she was already farther out, at Spiegel's house. So she just crossed the road."

"If it was an accident." Maybe I was too used to dealing with murders. A burglary, even at a sperm bank, seemed tame. Boring. My imagination was creating more mystery than there really was. I told that to Rosie too.

She sighed. "Then we need to talk to those Hackman kids, get them to admit they stole the sperm, and go home."

"We're playing poker tonight."

"Then we'll go home tomorrow." She was laughing at me. I grinned back at her. Sometimes I wish we were both heterosexual. Sometimes I wonder if we've been able to get this close because she isn't.

We turned back along the beach, walking close to the water. I spotted Melody's pink pajamas up on the dunes, headed back to the spit, and waved. She waved back. Fifteen minutes later we hiked up the path to the road.

Rosie started the truck, put it in gear, and pulled off the shoulder, heading toward town.

We were about to hit the first sharp curve at about thirty-five miles an hour, and I couldn't help but notice that she wasn't slowing down. Then I noticed that she was riding the brake and we still weren't slowing down.

I felt my heart lurch, and I gagged on the baseball that had suddenly sprouted in my throat.

Rosie was wrestling with the wheel. The curve went on and on, and I wasn't sure what the incline below us was like, how far down it went, how steep it was. There was no guard rail. Still struggling to steer, Rosie clawed at the hand brake blindly. I threw my left arm in front of Alice, on the seat between us, and braced my right arm on the dash. I wasn't breathing. Rosie was keening, a high-pitched wail of concentration, yanking at the hand brake.

We almost made it. Three-quarters of the way around the endless curve we slid sideways off the road, across the shoulder, across the tall green grass, and over the edge.

The truck landed on its side—my side, against tree trunks. I wasn't sure how far we'd fallen. It had felt like we'd been spinning off the road for twenty minutes. Alice was sitting on my shoulder, whining. My nose was running warm blood, although I didn't remember hitting it.

My right arm hurt like hell.

I could hear Rosie breathing. Then she said, "Are you okay?"

I coughed, and more blood bubbled out of my nose. "Yeah. You?"

"Okay."

I heard her yank at the door handle, and I heard the catch give, but she was having trouble getting the heavy door to move upward. "Shit. No leverage," she rasped. I turned my head, looking up past Alice, who looked alert, if confused, and saw Rosie's butt going through the open window. She disappeared. Then the door swung open. Alice, using me as a springboard, leaped up and out. Rosie reappeared, reaching down toward me. I stood on the smashed passenger-side door—my legs seemed okay—and let her help me up. I could have done it myself if my right arm had been working.

She helped me up to the road, too, which wasn't more than ten feet above the spot where the truck rested, against a stand of young eucalyptus that the gods must have planted. Because there was another twenty-foot drop to the dunes below, and twenty more feet could have done a lot of damage.

"You've got blood all over you," Rosie said.

"I know."

"And you can't use your arm."

"Are we going to stand here forever stating the obvious?" I grumped. "I think my nose has stopped bleeding."

"I'll go get help."

"I can walk perfectly well," I said. But at that moment I found myself sitting on the shoulder and I decided not to say anything else.

"Keep your head back. Sit tight. I'll get someone." She took off her jacket and put it over my shoulders. I did as I was told. I sat tight and watched Rosie and Alice trot off down the road.

—12—

It turned out that Rosie didn't have to run all the way into town. Marty Spiegel, returning from his shopping trip, spotted her on the road, picked her up, and took her to Clement's office. Clement called an ambulance and a wrecker, told them where to find the bodies this time, then followed the Jag back to where I still sat, head back, the nosebleed slowed to a trickle, the pain in my arm so massive I couldn't tell what part of the arm was actually damaged.

There was a game I'd played as a kid, when my anything-but-painless dentist was having at me, and I was playing it today. A game of history. The Inquisition Game. They were trying to convert me. I was stretched on a rack (or clamped into a thumbscrew, or tied to a stake on a pile of burning brush) but I was very brave and would not give in. My imaginings, then, had been so much worse than the reality that the pain of the dentist's drill had seemed trivial. The game wasn't working so well now. My arm really did feel like it was being ripped apart slowly, and I couldn't imagine the rack hurting more. Rosie's jacket wasn't keeping me warm. The afternoon fog was coming in, cold and wet, and I was shivering.

I was thinking about how cold I was getting—maybe I would go numb—when the Jag pulled up, spraying pebbles from its tires, followed by Clement.

Clement had a blanket, which he wrapped around me. I was going to tell him the blanket was unnecessary, but my teeth were chattering.

"What's hurt, son?" he asked. "I mean besides your nose?"

I hadn't even remembered that I had a nose. "Arm. I think the shoulder's all torn up. No big thing. No bones sticking out." He gave me a look that said, "Sure, tough guy," a look worthy of my own father.

The wrecker got there before the ambulance, which had to come from Rosewood, ten miles away. The driver was the same man we'd bought gas from a little while before, and now I remembered that I'd seen him once before. He was the old, sour-looking guy who had been the third man at the table with Henry and Perry, the table across from me that first day I'd eaten at Georgia's. He looked down at the truck, shaking his head. That's what they do when they're going to charge you too much. He hadn't done a lot more than that by the time the ambulance arrived.

I told Rosie I would understand if she wanted to stay with her truck. She said the man with the wrecker would see to the truck, thanks anyway, and she and Spiegel would go along to the hospital.

Clement said Frank—the guy with the wrecker—was going to need some help. He'd stay with him.

The hospital was big and modern and the emergency room wasn't too crowded. It wasn't long before my nose was pronounced unbroken and my shoulder dislocated.

Rosie admitted to a crick in her neck, which the young doctor said was a crick in the neck.

The Rosewood veterinarian confirmed our diagnosis. The dog was fine.

Marty dropped us off at the police station, and took his groceries home. Clement was there, and gave us what he knew about the truck. It had a broken axle, a smashed muffler, a twisted drive shaft, a wrecked fender and passenger-side door, a front bumper ripped off, and a lot of dings. The brakes had failed, he said, because the lines had "come loose" from the master cylinder.

"Come loose?" Rosie objected. "Those nuts don't just fall off. And the brakes were fine when we drove up there."

He nodded, thoughtful. "Or someone took 'em off," he

agreed. "Ground was soaked with fluid where you said you'd parked."

He offered us a ride the short distance to the motel and we took it. I swallowed a pain pill and went to bed. Rosie went outside, and returned half an hour later. She'd been checking out the Chevy.

"Everything looks okay," she said. "The well's full, the brake lines are in one piece. No burning torch sticking out of the gas tank."

I heard her say something about "doing a few things" right before I dozed off.

— *13* —

Rosie was moving around in the next room. I looked at the clock. Two hours had passed. I called out, and she came in.

"I brought back some food," she said. "Hungry?"

"Sure."

She had been doing more than going for takeout. She had gone to the Hackman's, where she had found the younger of the two boys, Tommy, at home alone. He was about fourteen, she said. He wouldn't let her in, but she did her best Nancy Drew act and got him curious enough to agree to talk to her out in the yard. She told me about their conversation over a dinner of gooey hot turkey sandwiches on Styrofoam bread on Styrofoam plates, which we ate sitting on my bed.

She had started out by telling the boy that we were investigative reporters, and that her partner had been injured in a "suspicious accident." We felt, she told him, that something very odd was going on in Wheeler, and that someone had tried to get us because we had been looking into the break-in at the bank, and the death of Gracie Piedmont.

Rosie described Tommy as a bright, nervous, sly-eyed kid,

tall for his age, physically clumsy, and self-conscious in her presence.

He had demanded to know exactly what she wanted from him.

She told him that we'd heard his older brother, Rollie, had been the one who had found the bank's assets out on the beach the morning after the burglary, and that we were wondering if he'd seen anything else.

"How would I know?" the kid said.

"What did you think when you found out what had happened?"

He tried to be cool, but he wasn't handling it very well, she said. He grinned and blustered and picked at a hangnail and told her he thought the break-in was "pretty dumb" and the bank itself was "weird."

"Some of the people in town," she said, "think you and your brother might have pulled the job."

He had laughed—proudly, she thought—and admitted that they had a reputation, all right.

He wouldn't say they'd done it—and he wouldn't say they hadn't done it. And he didn't know where his brother was or when he'd be home.

I was having trouble eating with my left hand, and dropped a gob of mashed potatoes and gravy on the front of my clean shirt. It slithered down to my lap.

"What's the house like?"

"Poor. The yard's a mess. There's an old station wagon on blocks in the side yard."

"What do you think?" I maneuvered a slice of turkey into my mouth.

"Hard to tell with a kid like that. Maybe they did do it. But then again, it's possible he just wants to give the impression of guilt. Their reputation, you know. We need to talk to his brother. And his parents."

Rosie had made two more calls while I'd been sleeping.

She had invited Nora to the poker game, but didn't think she'd come because she had said something about wanting to work. Rosie had then dropped by Melody Clift's house and invited her. Melody said she'd be delighted. An interesting group: Clement, Spiegel, Melody Clift, Perry, and us.

I decided to skip the pain pills for the evening so I could be awake and alert for the poker game. Beer's a pretty good painkiller, anyway.

My arm was heavily bandaged, set in a sling. I couldn't quite manage a shower, so I sponged myself down and put on clean clothes, once again.

Rosie drove the Chevy. As a teenager I'd had a lot of practice at driving a shift car with my left hand while the right was otherwise occupied, but that had been a long, long time ago, and I didn't feel like trying it just yet.

Clement's house was a small stucco bungalow, a couple of blocks from the center of town. Pale green with white trim. Maybe twelve hundred square feet, maybe a little more. It had a shallow front porch with barely enough room for two redwood chairs with plastic cushions and a small redwood table between them that held a jade plant in a clay burro planter. The concrete stairs and porch were freshly painted in that terra-cotta color they sell for concrete. The front yard was two small patches of carefully tended lawn, with rhododendrons up against the house.

The front door was much newer than the rest of the house, one of those carved, Spanish-style numbers they sell in places like Sears and Montgomery Ward. It had a brass knocker. A horseshoe.

When Clement opened the door, we stepped directly into a beige-carpeted living room painted a soft rose, and were invited to sit on a beige and gold brocade couch backed up against a side wall and facing a large white-draped window. Clement disappeared through a small dining room into the kitchen and we looked around the room. There were several large plants, including a five-foot palmetto in one corner and a large rectangular planter of asparagus fern against the arch-cut wall dividing living room from dining room.

It was a while before I noticed that the palmetto was populated by several small plastic birds, and that nestled in the asparagus fern were a foot-tall mother monkey with child, glazed pottery of some sort.

The wall behind us and above our heads was covered with photographs, family photographs that spanned at least four generations, framed and arranged, or so it seemed, chronologically from sepia Victorian formality to infant in paper diapers. Clement came back into the room, bearing a tray of cheese and crackers, chips and onion dip, and beer, which he set down on the glass-topped coffee table before us.

The house was very clean, very neat, but Clement's presence was comfortable, so I wasn't afraid of dropping crumbs. Come to think of it, the place didn't look much like it belonged to Clement, who tended toward a rumpled look.

"Noticed you looking at the pictures," he said. "That's my wife up there." He pointed over our heads. "The wedding picture. That's me in the uniform."

World War II. A young soldier, a corporal, with a silly, glazed grin on his face. A young bride in white, with shoulder-length rolled-under and pompadoured blond hair. Dark eyebrows, dark lipstick, looking happy but exhausted, or possibly frightened.

At last, their faces seemed to say, they would get to go to bed together.

"She's beautiful," I said, although that wasn't strictly true. She was pretty, but it's always hard to tell how good-looking someone from another era really is. The style, even the bearing, get in the way.

"Yes, she was. Right up to the day she died."

"When was that, Clement?" Rosie asked. I didn't want to know.

"Been nearly two years now." He was gazing at the photos. "Stroke. Just took her away. She died in our bedroom early in the morning. I couldn't decide what she should be dressed in . . . but you don't want to hear that." We murmured things just below the level of real speech.

"Quite a collection of pictures though, isn't it? Both our families, way back."

Dutifully, we turned again, twisting our bodies to look up at the wall. He started with the Victorians on his side, who, he said, had lived in Oregon. My neck was getting stiff and I didn't need to have anything else hurting, so I stood up. From the Victorians, he introduced us to the flaming youth, and then the serious folk of the Depression. World War II, his own wedding, and, in the years right after the war, what seemed to be dozens of relatives all living in little houses and multiplying like crazy. His own son as a baby, a fifties child, a long-haired student in Berkeley in the sixties. Clement and his wife, Rita, growing middle-aged and then beginning to get old. No more photos of them after that. Two grandchildren, a boy and a girl, rushing toward their teens. Another picture of the grandson, the infant in paper diapers.

The tour was finished. Clement sat down. I sat down.

"Nice house," Rosie said, to change the subject.

"It's just the way she left it," he said. "I haven't changed much. She was the decorator in the family. Hell, I work most of the time, anyway. Hardly live here."

I remembered, then, that he was looking for something to do when he finally retired. I realized how important it would be for him to find it.

Perry was the first to arrive, carrying a twist-cap jug of wine.

"You drinking, Clement?" he asked, waving the bottle at his boss.

"Not anymore." Clement took a last swig from his beer.

"The town has to have one sober peacekeeper more or less on duty."

Perry nodded agreeably, went to the kitchen, and came back clutching a tumbler of cheap red.

We decided to wait for a fifth player to arrive before we began. Clement began counting out chips at the dining room table. I waited until Perry had swallowed half his wine, and then brought up the events of the night before.

"That's really something," I said, "the way you thought to look over the edge of the cliff."

"Believe me," he chortled, "it was the last place I looked. I wasn't too eager to go out there and hang off the lip, looking for Gracie."

"What did you do first," Rosie said, "when you got the call?" She sounded all breathless with admiration and wonder.

"Well, first I spotted the car, of course. Went to Spiegel's to look for her, where she was supposed to be. And spotted the car in the drive. So then I tromped all around the house, yelling like a fool in the wind. Damned near got beaned by a tree limb too."

"And then?" I prodded.

He took a long swallow, nearly emptying his glass. "Checked the houses right around, of course. Henry's, next door, and Melody's. No sign of anyone, no sign of Gracie. Excuse me." He got up and went to the kitchen again, returning with a second water glass full of wine. He took a long pull and plunked himself down in his chair, his round face shining with pride. "Now, where were we? Okay, so I checked all around, yelled, looked around the yards. She just wasn't nowhere around there, so I crossed the road. The waves were splashing up pretty good, coming right up over the top every so often. I timed them. Took my chance, and looked over the edge. I can tell you, it was something." He paused for approval, and both Rosie and I nodded admiringly. "There she was, down there on the rocks, those waves pulling her—well, trying to pull her, but she was jammed in pretty good. Still, I was scared we'd lose her."

"Hell of a job, finding her like that," I said.

"I got three dollars each here to start," Clement yelled from the dining room. "Think that's about right?"

We said we thought it was.

Marty Spiegel was next to appear, wearing the same jeans and plaid shirt he'd been wearing earlier that day. I was glad to see I hadn't bled on him. He greeted Clement and Perry as if he were glad to see them, smiled sweetly at Rosie, patted the dog, and asked how I was feeling.

"No problem," I lied. We all moved into the dining room, paid our three dollars, and took our chips.

Clement rummaged in a drawer and found the cards.

"There seems to be an awful lot going on around here these days, Clement. Must be keeping you busy," Spiegel said.

Clement shook his head. "Yeah. Too damned much."

"Yeah," Perry said. Then he squinted like Clint Eastwood and added, "But you just try to get your teeth into any of it and it's like biting into . . . well, wine." He finished his second glass and poured more.

Clement glared at him. I didn't know whether it was for the comment or the drinking.

There was a knock on the door, and Clement went to answer. Melody Clift swept in and rushed to my good side.

"You poor thing! Rosie told me there was an accident. Imagine, right after I talked to you on the beach. How very terrible. What happened exactly?"

"Brakes failed," Clement said tersely, but he was gazing at her with some approval. Which wasn't hard to do. She was wearing a flowered blouse in blue and lavender, and tight lavender pants. The blouse showed cleavage for days, and very nice cleavage it was too. In artificial light she looked younger than she had on the beach. She was one of those superfeminine women I don't usually feel drawn to. I tend to date lawyers and journalists. Like Lee. Still, I thought, appreciating Melody's softness, it wasn't like I was engaged or anything.

We drew for the deal. Rosie got it, and started out slow with five-card draw, guts to open. Melody, sitting next to me, said she would be glad to put my chips in the pot, since I was playing one-handed. I thanked her and accepted the offer. Rosie was trying not to grin, and failing in the effort.

She dealt me the two, seven, and nine of spades, a six of diamonds, and a jack of clubs. I tossed in the six and the jack, hoping feebly for more spades. I was amazed when I actually got them. A ten and a four. I took the pot with no trouble at all.

Clement dealt next, seven-card stud, deuces wild. I folded after four unimpressive cards, and watched Melody play it out. She had, when the fourth up card was dealt, a pair of jacks, a five, and a deuce showing. Everyone but Spiegel folded. He raised her dime bet to twenty cents and lost, holding three kings to her jacks-over-fives full house.

It was interesting, watching her play. She gave nothing away, and she milked the other players carefully, never raising so much that she scared them out early. Soft, maybe, but a good poker player.

When the deal passed to Perry, who was flushed with wine, he called spit in the ocean. Once again Clement glared at him. Spiegel looked like he thought the reference was in bad taste. I wasn't sure, looking at Perry, whether he meant anything by it at all.

The up card was a four. I had another one in my hand. Two wild cards. And a queen of hearts and ten of diamonds. And a five. Three queens, at least, and a possible, though not likely, straight. This was one of those games where four of a kind tends to be the winner. My hand was not terrific. Enough to stay in, not enough to count on.

I decided to start out by bluffing, raising the nickel bet to a dime first round. In the draw I asked for one card. I got the ten of spades. Not bad at all. I raised the bet to twenty cents. Rosie, Clement, Marty, and Perry all folded, stunned by my confidence. Melody studied my face and raised me a quarter. I guess people don't get rich by being passive, not even romance writers. But what the hell, maybe she had a full house or four twos. I called, and raised her another quarter. She laughed and saw my quarter.

She was holding a pair of fours and a pair of sixes—five sixes with the common wild card. Five.

We played a few more hands, and then Spiegel jumped to his feet and said to deal him out, he wanted to stretch his legs outside for a few minutes. I went with him.

Walking wasn't great, because it jarred my arm, but I wanted to get to know him, and a crowd wasn't the best place to do that. He walked slowly, which surprised me and made me think maybe he was matching his pace to my wounds.

"Tell me what it's like to be a detective, Jake," he said after we'd walked for a couple of minutes.

I laughed. "Look at me. Arm in a sling, nose swollen. That's what it's like."

He shook his head. "No, come on. Why do you do it if that's all there is?"

"Hell, Marty, I just kind of fell into it. It seemed to be something I was pretty good at, I got a couple of requests from people to help them . . . it worked. I like figuring things out, tracking things down. When I was a kid I thought I wanted to be a cop. I was for a while, in Chicago."

"When was that?"

"One of the years was 1968."

He stopped and leaned against a tree. "Your arm's bothering you. Let's stop for a minute. You were there in '68? As a cop? Jesus."

"Why, were you there as something else?"

"No. I was pretty young, and I was no yippie, anyway. I didn't have much interest in the democratic convention, or in any kind of politics. I was an L.A. kid, hanging around Venice, writing poetry. Is that why you're not a cop now? The '68 riots?"

"Yeah. I hit a kid in the head with my stick and his friends carried him away. Maybe he was an asshole, maybe he was a decent, idealistic kid. I think the people that led him there knew what they were getting him into, because everyone knew the cops were assholes, and the mayor was an asshole . . ." I realized I was going on and on. "I left. Left the force, left Chicago. Came out here and bummed around, got into this and that. And wound up being a kind of cop anyway. By the way, Clement thinks Rosie and I are just reporters. We've got a tie-in with *Probe* magazine, so in a way it's true, okay?"

I was taking a big chance trusting him with the information, but I couldn't see that there would be anything in it for him one way or the other. Even if he were a killer.

"Sure. Whatever you say. Just don't end up quoting me in some stupid article."

"Promise. Whatever happened to the poetry?"

"Well, I was going to be a poet, then I took this course in astrology, and that kind of changed things."

We were walking again, back toward the house. He continued. "One day I was able to read my own chart and I saw something in it that scared me." He hesitated. "An early death. I suppose you think that's bullshit."

"I didn't know you could see things like that in a chart."

He shrugged. "I saw it in mine. And suddenly a life of artistic poverty didn't seem so wonderful. I decided the best defense against death was money, and I decided—also according to my chart—that movies were the way to make it."

"You still think you're going to die young?"

"I don't know anymore. But I'm putting things by for that eventuality."

I had to ask. "Like at the sperm bank?"

He laughed. "Could be."

We'd been gone only a few minutes, but Rosie's stacks had grown. Melody gave me a big smile and asked if I wanted her to pour me another beer. Yes, I said, and thanks.

I noticed when I sat down that her chair had crept closer to mine, so that our thighs were half an inch apart. The slightest twitch and we'd be touching. Fun, I thought. Too bad my arm feels like a bag of screaming nerves. And the thought of kissing someone and accidentally bumping noses was almost more than I could stand.

I tried concentrating on the play, and on the players. Clement had been right about Perry. He played stupid. But he was interesting to watch as part of the group. He was easy with Clement, shy with Melody, and deferential to the point of insult with Spiegel. He called him Mr. Spiegel, stiffly. I couldn't tell whether he was afraid of the man or disliked him.

We played until eleven-thirty, when Clement, noticing that Perry was nodding off, told us to go on playing while he took his sodden employee home. Marty stayed for a while. When he left, Rosie took Alice outside for a walk, leaving me alone with Melody.

She shared a last beer with me.

"You don't feel very well, do you, Jake?"

"Rotten," I admitted.

"Well, of course. Poor baby. I'll just finish this little bit of beer and go right home. But you must promise to come and visit me soon."

"Tomorrow."

She kissed me in a sisterly fashion, on the cheek.

Rosie and Alice came back in, followed by Clement. Melody announced her departure, and we all agreed it was time to stop.

—14—

The arm kept me awake until about three A.M., when I gave up and dropped some pain pills.

Rosie let me sleep until ten. I tried to ignore her loud fidgeting in the next room, but the message was clear: it was time for breakfast, time for work.

The hot turkey sandwich the night before had put me off Georgia's, and I didn't feel like eating a giant, greasy omelet, anyway. We went back to the Santa Rosa Plum, the sprout-and-avocado place, where bran muffins got top billing on the breakfast menu.

It was nearly empty. I was beginning to wonder how the town survived every winter. We took a booth and began to plan our day, but we hadn't gotten far when the waitress, the same tired-looking woman who had waited on us the day before, dumped a couple of menus on the table and said "Good morning" in an unfriendly voice.

I looked up at her, startled. "When you decide what you want," she said, "I want to talk to you."

"Sure," Rosie said. "About what?"

"About my son Tommy, that's what."

I was touched. Strangers knew us by sight. Nothing like a small town. We glanced at the menus, ordered muffins, orange juice, and coffee. She went to get them, and, when she returned with our orders, pulled up a chair at the end of our booth. I could tell this was going to be very good for the digestion, especially after her first few words.

"You got a lot of nerve, you media people," she said. "Sneaking around and talking to kids when they're all alone."

"We didn't know he'd be all alone," Rosie said reasonably.

"But he was. Now suppose you tell me what this is all about."

My sore shoulder did not make me a more charming and agreeable person, but I tried.

"Possibly you know, Mrs. Hackman, that there are rumors around town that your boys might have been involved in a prank over at the cryobank."

"Why would reporters care about that? What kind of story are you after, anyway?"

I studied her. She had that look people get when they've worked too long at tedious jobs for too little money. She couldn't have been more than thirty-five or forty, but her long brown hair looked undernourished, drained. It wouldn't comb properly and had no real color. Her face was pale and her skin looked dry. Her blue eyes sat deep in premature crepe. She was slightly overweight and gone to sag. And she looked really pissed off.

"We're just interested in finding out what happened over there," I told her. "You have to admit it's an odd story. Maybe it was a kid's prank and maybe it wasn't."

She looked doubtful. A couple of new customers came in and she got up to give them menus. Then she came back and sat down again.

"I think you should leave my kids out of it. They're good boys."

Yeah, I thought. That's what everybody always said about mass murderers.

"So you don't think they had anything to do with it?" I asked unnecessarily. "Then what do you think happened?"

She snorted. "Maybe someone didn't like the merchandise they got or something. Or it was religious, like I heard. Maybe someone had it in for Nora Canfield. But my kids were home all night, in bed. I know that." Bullshit, I thought. There wasn't a kid in the world who couldn't sneak out of the house and sneak back in again with enough motivation.

"Why do you think people would suspect them of it, then?" Rosie asked.

"People. What do they know? The boys had a few problems a couple of years ago. They're high-spirited. You know boys. If Clement Paisley can't solve a crime, that's his problem, not mine." The new customers called out to her and she went to take their order. She came back again. We had started on our second muffins.

"You've got to admit," Rosie said, swallowing, "that it looks like a kid's prank."

"No, it does not. What about that note? Religious nuts. We got a couple of those in this town, let me tell you."

"Got any candidates?" I asked.

"You can just bet I do. I know you talked to Fredda. You meet that kid of hers? You go talk to the kid's great-aunt, that Hilda Carlson. And while you're at it, talk to Frank Wooster, over at the garage. He's been pals with Hilda for thirty years. You maybe should talk to Joanne too. But not my kids. They're okay. They don't do burglary."

After much sympathetic listening to her list of alternate suspects—at one point she mentioned Wolf, and even Perry—she agreed to let us stop over that night when her whole family would be home and get the boys' side of things. Maybe, she said, they would have some ideas too.

I wasn't looking forward to it, but meeting the family was a good way to get a real line on the kids.

She finally left us alone. We finished our coffee and got out of there.

Our first stop was the garage, to see if the mechanic could tell us any more about the accident and to take a second look at the mechanic himself.

He was under the truck. He eased himself out, and spoke to me, ignoring Rosie. "Mr. Samson, I sure can't tell how those lines came loose."

"The truck belongs to my friend," I said, nodding at Rosie. He acted like that put a new perspective on the problem, and turned to her abruptly.

"You need to take more care with it," he told her. "Get it checked out once in a while, make sure everything's screwed on tight. You got to maintain a vehicle."

"I do," Rosie said. "It was fine. Something happened."

"Vehicles don't just do things like that," he argued. "It's like someone opened up that hood and pulled them nuts right off." Once again he was talking to me, man to man, about Rosie's obviously neglected and mismanaged truck.

Up until this point Rosie had taken his attitude in stride, but she was beginning to lose her sense of humor.

"Maybe that's exactly what happened—if that's what it looks like," she snapped.

He frowned at the truck. "Well, that's what it looked like, all right. You can ask Clement and Perry. They was here to check it out. And I didn't touch no part of it beforehand, either." He scratched his gray stubble. "You think maybe someone done this on purpose, Mr. Samson? For a joke or something like that?"

The prank theory of crime seemed popular in this town.

"Not much of a joke," I said.

He pursed his thin lips and gazed straight at me with icy blue eyes.

"Makes a good story," he said.

Rosie was staring at him, dumbstruck. But I was cool.

"Don't you think it would be kind of stupid to commit suicide for a story that someone else would have to write?"

His eyes skipped away from me again. He didn't want to call me stupid outright. "Maybe," he said, gazing out the door, "someone got irritated. That can happen when you go around looking for things, annoying people."

"We had no idea we were annoying anyone," Rosie said, all wide brown eyes. "Why would anyone be irritated with us?"

He shook his head, smiling ruefully. "Maybe you just

rubbed someone the wrong way. Some people around here think the burglar did a good thing."

"Do you?"

"I obey the law. About the truck," he said, turning to me again, "I got to wait for some parts before I can get this altogether fixed. Got a body man can't work on it until Tuesday. If you need to get back to the city, you'll have to come back and get it later. Can't be helped."

"Oh, that's okay," Rosie said. "It looks like we'll be around for a while." The estimate figure was, of course, immense. Rosie told me that she had a five-hundred-dollar deductible. I said we'd have to get that from our employer.

—15—

Once again there was no answer at Nora's house, so I tried her office. Sure enough, she was there.

"You missed a great poker game last night."

"I probably should have taken the evening off. I think I'm spinning my wheels today. Speaking of which, I heard about your accident."

"It was no accident." I told her about Rosie's deductible after I told her about the disconnected brake lines. She said she'd pay.

"Is everyone else there working too?"

"No. I'm the only one who came in today. You can expect people to put in overtime on Saturday, but Sunday . . ."

"We need to talk to your employees, see what we can get. Someone might know something, some small piece that will lead us somewhere."

"I suppose that would have to be tomorrow, then. It will really cut into the workday, but I suppose you have to."

"Yes. We do. We'll be there in the morning sometime. Another thing. You've got family in town, right?"

"Yes, why?"

"Where can we find them?"

"Why?"

Jesus, she could be tiresome. "There could be any number of reasons for the burglary," I explained. "We can't rule out someone having a personal grudge against you or someone close to you. They might know something you don't. It's just routine."

I hated to fall back on cop talk, but I was tired of answering questions. I wanted to ask some. She gave me the phone number of the aunt and uncle who had raised her. I thanked her, said we'd see her the next day, and hung up.

Her aunt and uncle were home, and gave me directions to the house. They lived at the extreme edge of town, as far away from the ocean as you could get and still be in Wheeler.

These were the people who had brought her up when her own parents had died. They were her mother's sister and brother-in-law. They were in their sixties, retired from whatever it was they had done before.

Unlike so many of the houses we'd seen in Wheeler, theirs was freshly painted, white with French-blue trim. Carpenter gothic, small, with carving on the eaves. The front yard was perfect, which is no small feat in January in northern California. Someone had been keeping the grass down and the weeds away. The hedge was trimmed. Even the birches in the front yard looked tidy. Not a branch out of place anywhere, despite the recent storm.

Mrs. Dorfmann answered the door with a sweet smile and a charming welcome. She had, she said, just made some coffee cake, and she hoped we'd join them in the kitchen. We followed her through the house, through a cozy, overstuffed living room and small dining room, and into a large kitchen that had been completely remodeled and equipped with shiny new appliances, expensive-looking cabinets, and, judging by the food processor which must have raised real estate values on the block, the latest and best doodads.

Mrs. Dorfmann looked around the room, puzzled. "He was here a few minutes ago. He won't hear me if I shout," she fretted. "I wonder, Mr. Samson, if you'd go out in the yard and find my husband while Rosie and I set the table."

I didn't dare look at Rosie.

As directed, I went out the back door. The elderly gentleman, his back to me, was puttying a new pane of glass on a homemade cold frame constructed of two-by-fours and window frames. A large cold frame or a small greenhouse, about two by three by six.

Assuming from what his wife had said that his hearing was not perfect, I took great care not to sneak up on him. I approached him from the side, then circled around so he could see me coming, which he finally did. I smiled. He smiled. "Time for coffee cake," I said in a hearty baritone. He didn't seem to have any trouble hearing me, and when he spoke, it was at normal volume.

"Perfect," he said. "I'm hungry."

Just thinking about homemade coffee cake was having the same effect on me, so I was a little disenchanted when I noticed the plastic wrapper with a familiar brand name lying on the sink. Still, the cake was hot. That was something.

"You wanted to talk to us about Nora?" Dorfmann asked. "What exactly did you want to know and why?"

"She couldn't think of anyone who might want to harm her business," Rosie said. "It occurred to us that her family might be able to fill things in a little."

"I can't imagine why anyone would want to do her any harm," Mrs. Dorfmann protested. "Not many people in this town have a child like Nora. It was hard, when her parents died—in a car crash, it was—because we didn't have any money and there we were with a child to raise. But Nora was always finding little jobs around town, always bringing something in to help out, even when she was a child. Even when she went down to the City, she'd send us presents, useful things we needed. When Bernard retired from the nursery we didn't have anything to live on but social security, and here he'd had his heart attack and everything."

"Is that when she came back, when he had the heart attack?" Rosie asked.

"Not long after," Mrs. Dorfmann continued. "I don't know what we'd have done without her. She's certainly paid us back for raising her. Now you could say she's raising us. She takes care of everything. We never have to worry. Isn't that right, Bernard?" He didn't respond. "Bernard?" She repeated what she'd said.

Dorfmann nodded, and shoved a huge chunk of coffee cake into his mouth. "Wonderful child, wonderful girl," he said, spraying crumbs.

The conversation pretty much went on like that. We complimented them on their house and got praise for Nora, who kept it in good repair. We complimented them on their yard and got praise for Nora, who had hired and paid for a weekly gardener.

I asked about Wolf. "He must have been pretty disappointed when she left town."

Mrs. Dorfmann laughed. "He sure was. But you know men." She winked at Rosie. "He got over it fast. Couldn't have the one he loved, loved the one he got next." Dorfmann, too, laughed, and, fortunately, had nothing in his mouth at the time.

We kept trying for a while, but we got the same answers over and over again, and the coffee was giving me heartburn. We finally left, with a lying promise to return sometime.

16

We were walking down Main when we ran into Clement, who was coming out of a doorway beside the grocery store.

"That's pretty much it for Gracie's effects," he said.

"I don't mean to sound dumb," I said, "but what are you talking about?"

"Gracie. You know, the dead woman?"

"Yes, we know the dead woman."

He laughed. "That's her apartment up there." He jerked a thumb toward the apartment upstairs of the grocery. "Was. I closed the place up when she died. Went over everything— just in case. Nothing to find. Fredda's up there now, picking over the corpse." He was eyeing me sardonically. "What's the matter, Jake? You're looking kind of surprised. Didn't you expect me to do what I could to follow up? Like I say, just in case?"

I denied it. I was torn between kicking myself for neglecting that part of the dead woman's private life and being glad that Clement had done it. I was beginning to think that if this man said there was nothing to find, there might not be anything to find.

"Have you got some time, Clement?" Rosie asked. "We need to get more information about the people who live on the spit. The ones we don't know about yet."

"Matter of fact, I don't. Got a family thing over in Rosewood, won't get back until later this afternoon. How about then?" She said that would be fine.

My arm was bothering me, so we picked up sandwiches at Georgia's and walked back toward the motel, laying plans for the day.

I reminded Rosie that I had promised to visit Melody.

"There's a lot I want to talk to her about—her neighbors, for one thing. And see if I can't get her to remember seeing something on the beach yesterday. I know she doesn't think she did, but who knows? Maybe she remembered something at three o'clock this morning."

"Sure, Jake. And I'm sure you want to do that alone, so I'll deal with things here in town. Checking on Wolf, for instance."

I ignored her smirking attitude. We agreed to meet back at the motel in time for dinner. Rosie ate her sandwich and took off. I gave myself half a pain pill and half an hour in bed, thinking. Then I got into the Chevy and drove out to the spit.

When I drove past Marty's place, I spotted his Jaguar halfway up the driveway and thought again about what part or parts he could have played in the week's events. He was involved with the sperm bank. He had asked Gracie to go out on the spit. And he could have followed us out of town, messed up the truck, driven back toward town, turned around and driven back again, a while later, to see what had happened. And there was Rosie, walking the road looking for help. He couldn't very well ride on by. Besides, he'd want to know if we'd gotten scared enough, or if I'd been badly enough injured, to pull out of town.

It wouldn't be the first time someone I'd liked had turned out bad. I was hoping, though, that Rosie would come up with something against Wolf. Where was he when Gracie died? And the truck crash—we knew he was at the tavern earlier that day. Was he there all afternoon?

Melody's house was redwood and glass, like Marty's, but only the materials were the same. If Hans Christian Andersen had moved to the Sonoma coast, he might have built a house like this one.

The main floor was a big hexagon, with large hexagonal windows on either side of the doorway. The door itself was carved with flowers and flanked by carved columns. The second floor got more elaborate. Dormers and eaves all over the place, each with scrollwork gingerbread and all jutting out from the parent hexagon in various directions, creating, I thought, what must be some interestingly shaped rooms. Rising from that confusing second story was a tower, also hexagonal, that made me think of sleeping beauties and ladders made of yellow hair. There should have been flags flying somewhere.

It took about thirty seconds for Melody to answer the door. She had been waiting for me, she explained, but she had been up in her study working, just until I arrived.

"Is your study in the tower?" I asked.

"No," she said. "That's the bedroom."

She was wearing a shiny pink robe, full length, with white lace peeking out of the bosom and fluffy mules peeking out from under the hem. This was fun, I thought. Like walking in on the star of a 1952 movie. The house wasn't quite right, but she was.

She led me into an immense living room with an immense fieldstone fireplace in which someone had laid an immense fire to drive away the foggy chill of the day. The fireplace was set into the lower level of the split-level room, a snug area with a pink semi-circle of a couch and red, pink, and white pillows. The carpeting was white, an alien concept that goes better with condos in Miami or the homes of L.A.'s conspicuous consumers than it does with the rugged, natural, and, therefore, dirty northern California coast. She sat me down on the couch, against some pillows, asked how my arm was feeling, and offered me a drink.

I accepted a glass of white wine. She went to a glitzy wet bar at the upper end of the room, poured my wine, and mixed herself something with gin in it. Over my left shoulder, through a glass wall, I watched eucalyptus trees swaying and parting to reveal a view of gray winter ocean. I looked back at the fire. She brought my wine and sat down next to me.

"Quite a house," I said.

She laughed. "I worked with the architect. He thought I was insane, but it was so much fun. I just let my imagination fly. I love doing that." She smiled at me. I smiled back. "Perhaps you'd like to see the rest of it later?"

"That would be nice."

"Now, then," she said, settling in beside me more closely. "You wanted to talk to me about some things, I believe?"

I nodded. "You came up here yesterday, isn't that right?" She said it was. "How much do you stay here—have you been around at all in the past couple of weeks?"

She didn't ask me why I wanted to know. She seemed to assume my questions were asked for reasonable purposes, and answered easily and to the point.

"I'm rarely here in the winter. I stay in my house in San Francisco unless I'm traveling. I've been holed up there since October working on a book. I came out yesterday because I was concerned about the house. And curious, too, I suppose, about the accident."

"You heard about it before yesterday?"

"My neighbor called and told me."

"Someone who lives here on the spit?"

"Yes. Henry Linton. Have you met Henry?"

"Man who owns the tavern?"

She laughed. "The tavern, one of the restaurants, a movie theater in Santa Rosa, half the real estate in town. He's also the mayor. Yes, that's Henry."

"I didn't know Wheeler had a king."

"Oh, nothing like that. He's a kind, quiet man. Anyway, he's my neighbor on this side." She gestured out toward the point of the spit. "He called to tell me the storm was causing some damage and I might want to check on the house. And he also told me about the Piedmont woman."

"Did he say how he found out?" I remembered that Angie had told him, but I didn't know the circumstances.

"As a matter of fact, he did. He'd gone over to Clement's office to find out if they were going to keep an eye on things out here that night. He had to stay in town and work, and he was worried about his house. No one was there but Angie, and she told him where Clement and Perry were. And why."

"Did you know Gracie Piedmont?"

She shook her head. "I know only a few people in town. Merchants, mostly, and people who live near me."

"Was there any damage to your house?"

"There's still the tree in the swimming pool. Once that's out, the pool will need some repair."

"I guess you assumed there'd be damage?"

She gave me a mildly irritated smile. "What do you mean?"

"You said you were upstairs working on a book today. I suppose that means you brought a manuscript or some notes or something with you, expecting to get stuck up here."

She laughed. "I have a deadline. I take it nearly everywhere. I don't have time for a day off right now."

"What can you tell me about some of the other people who live here?" She had gotten up to get us fresh drinks, and when she sat back down again she rested a casual hand on my shoulder.

"You know Marty, of course, but there are only a few permanent year-round residents. Henry is one." She described the other permanent residents. An elderly couple, retired. He had been an executive with the Sierra Club. They were involved in antiwhaling work, she said, and various other ecological causes. They had lived in Berkeley before they'd bought a lot on the spit and put up a "small jewel of a house."

A poet or something, she said, lived farther inland. An elderly woman who kept to herself. "Friendly enough when she sees you, but odd, I think. As though something happened to her once that was so devastating that she no longer wants much human companionship."

Well, I thought, Melody did write romances.

Then there was Frank Wooster.

Surprised, I said, "I wouldn't think the town mechanic would have enough money to build out here."

"The lot was in his family, and an old house that goes back, oh, forever. It's a wreck, really, but he lives in it. There are advantages to staying in the same place for five or six generations."

I laughed. "Or even two. But I wouldn't know about that."

The last of the permanent residents: a young couple in their thirties. He had made some big business killing in Silicon Valley or somewhere, had a heart attack, and now "dabbled in investments." She made "pots or lamps or something."

Of the part-time residents, besides herself and Marty, none of them, as far as she knew, had been out there at all since autumn and weren't likely to return until April or May.

She offered me another drink. The fire was making me feel very peaceful, and my arm actually seemed to be feeling better. I took another glass of wine from her rather pretty hand. Life was good.

"Tell me this, Melody. Are you sure you didn't see or hear anything around the beach the day our truck got booby-trapped? Anything, anyone at all?"

She rested the aforementioned hand again on my good shoulder.

"I think there were some people, way down the beach, nearer town. But I couldn't see them clearly."

"Male? Female?"

"I couldn't be sure. I'm sorry, Jake, but they were quite far away."

"You were up on the dunes. Were you up closer to the road? See any cars or anything?"

She shook her head, and ran a finger along my jaw. She moved closer.

"You didn't hear anything? Any voices or cars?"

She said she thought she remembered hearing a car or two passing along the road, but nothing distinctive, no odd sounds. Just cars. She asked where the truck had been parked and I told her, and she said she hadn't walked that far. She hadn't heard us crash.

Her hand was on the nape of my neck, moving into my scalp. "I like men with curly blond hair," she said. "I'll bet your neck is stiff, and your back," she said, "from holding your poor arm in place that way."

Yes, I admitted, I was feeling a little stiff.

"Why don't you lie down here?" She pointed at the white fur rug on the white carpeting between the couch and the fire. A white fur rug. I had never owned such a thing, and had never been invited by a woman to lie down on one. On other kinds of rugs, and other kinds of warm, soft places. But not a furry white rug.

"Is this real fur?" I asked, arranging myself on my stomach.

"Oh, no. I don't believe in that. I contribute heavily to the Fund for Animals."

She made me sit up again so she could help me off with my shirt. Then she went to a cabinet near the bar and came back carrying a jar of something.

"Skin cream," she said. "For your massage."

She sat beside me and began to work the cream into my spine, moving her fingers gently over the muscles around the shoulder blades, staying well away from the bandaged shoulder. She brought her thumbs up under my skull and pressed, then ran them down my neck and began to knead my back. My eyes were closed. I felt her move down, over my lower back, and sit astride my rump. She felt very, very warm. As she moved her hands over my back, she moved her body as well. And we both got very, very warm.

Then she slid down onto my thighs and began kneading my buttocks.

"If you're going to do that," I said, "I should probably take off my pants."

"Wonderful idea. Let me help you." Awkwardly, protecting my right shoulder, I turned over, then got to my feet. She looked me over, face to knees, and smiled. Then she unzipped my pants and peeled them off, along with my shorts. I didn't move. I stood still, watching her. She undid the sash of her robe, and a few buttons, and let it fall. It slithered down to the rug. She took my hand, moved up against me, and gave me one helluva kiss. The next thing I knew she was lying on the rug, laughing up at me.

Maybe this was a scene she'd written a dozen times before. Maybe this was what she'd been writing when I showed up that day. Maybe it was ridiculous, and not at all the sort of thing a real sophisticate would be caught dead doing. But I didn't keep her waiting.

There never was enough time, that day, to visit her hexagonal tower, which was too bad. On the other hand, there also wasn't enough time for her to read to me from her books, which was probably a good thing. I'm a mystery fan, myself.

—17—

Our walk to the Hackman house that evening after dinner took us past Fredda's house. The sky had cleared and the moon was bright, and a flash of light glinted off Joanne's wheelchair on the front porch. We waved and said hello. She said hello back.

While I'd been distressing my bad shoulder that afternoon, Rosie had picked up some interesting information. She'd found Henry Linton working the bar at the tavern and talked to him for a while. She'd come at things sideways, saying she'd expected to find Wolf there—didn't he work afternoons? She learned that he did, except for Sundays, when he worked just a couple of hours in the evening. He usually worked from noon to five, broke for dinner until six while Henry relieved him, then worked until eight or so, when Henry came in and worked until closing. On Fridays and Saturdays too? Yes. Which meant that unless there was something we didn't know, he'd worked all afternoon the day before, which put him out of the way as far as the truck was concerned. But it also meant he'd been taking his dinner break right around the time Gracie Piedmont had died.

She'd also visited the bookstore and talked to Lou Overman, who still insisted he'd slept through the break-in.

"So you believe him?"

"Why should I?" Obviously, Rosie was not enamored.

We compared notes on our spit-resident findings. What Rosie had learned from Clement narrowed things down considerably. The two couples—the Sierra Club folks and the young retiree and wife—had been gone at the time of Gracie's death. The old folks were visiting friends in Berkeley. The whiz kid and his spouse were in France. That left Henry, Frank, and the elderly poet.

"And Clement didn't get anything out of her, I suppose?"

"She was hiding out from the storm behind her shutters."

"We'll talk to her anyway, just in case."

The Hackmans lived just a few doors down from Fredda and Joanne. Rosie's description of poverty overwhelmed by its own debris was accurate. An old dismembered car in the weedy drive, an equally old but whole car parked in front. A house that looked as tired as Mrs. Hackman herself.

The man who opened the door was a big guy gone to seed. He was clutching a can of cheap beer and looking doubtfully at us from watery red eyes. Rosie offered to leave Alice outside.

He still looked doubtful. He didn't actually say hello, come on in. What he said was, "Dog's okay. My wife said you were coming." Then he jerked a thumb toward the interior and led the way into a living room full of sagging, stained beige nylon furniture.

Mrs. Hackman was sitting in front of the TV, which was tuned to the latest sex-and-violence-and-pseudo-history miniseries. With a look of resignation she turned it off and stood up.

"I'll get the boys," she said, and dragged wearily across the room to a door opening onto a pale pink hallway.

"Have a seat," Hackman said. "Can I offer you a beer?"

Looking around me at the furnishings that had probably come to the house second-hand, the tattered rug, I told him no, I wasn't thirsty. Beer, I suspected, was probably his big extravagance, and I thought I'd let him keep it to himself. Rosie, for maybe the same reason, said she was too full of dinner, but thanks anyway.

Mrs. Hackman returned, trailed by the fourteen-year-old Rosie had already met, and his older brother. Rosie's good at descriptions. I could have spotted Tommy on the street. Rollie Hackman looked like his father must have looked at sixteen. Large, strong, a little blurred, already, around the chin. His eyes were bright and alert, but I wouldn't call them friendly.

When we were all seated, the Hackmans waiting silently for someone to speak, my eye caught a glimpse of a watercolor painting on the wall behind the TV. I stood up again and walked closer to get a better look. The piece was badly matted and had no frame, but I recognized the work. It had been done by the same artist whose paintings and drawings I had admired at Overman's gallery.

"You like Rollie's work?" Mrs. Hackman asked.

"Very much." I took a longer look at the kid. His face was red, and he was looking at the floor. He still wasn't smiling. "I saw some of it at Overman's place when I first came to town. I thought it was the best stuff he had."

I enjoyed not having to lie to get people feeling cooperative, for once. At least I was hoping to get some cooperation.

"Rollie," Mr. Hackman said in a threatening voice.

"Thanks," the kid said. He was looking somewhere over my left shoulder, scratching the top of Alice's head. The dog seemed to find Rollie, of all the people in the room, particularly attractive.

"Sometimes people buy his stuff," Hackman said. His voice held an odd mixture of pride and fear. I guessed he didn't know what to do with his artistic son, knew he couldn't help him in any way, and wished he hadn't been "blessed" at all. "I guess he gets it from my wife's side."

"My grandmother was a milliner," she said. "She made beautiful hats. And she sewed too."

I decided against asking Hackman what he did for a living. Whatever it was, he wasn't terribly successful at it and didn't look like he was still trying.

"We don't want to take a lot of your time this evening," Rosie said, "and we're very grateful that you've allowed us to come and talk to you."

"That's okay," Mrs. Hackman said. "We want to set the record straight. Too many people are just too darned anxious to blame a poor man's kids for anything that goes on."

"I'm sure that's true," I agreed. I turned to Rollie. "Did you do it?"

"No." He looked directly at me, defiantly. For a kid, he was hard to read. There was something hidden there.

"Why do you think some people say you probably did?"

"Because me and Tommy got in trouble once, that's why."

Hackman broke in. "Couple years ago these two damned fools got themselves caught breaking into Frank's garage. Trying to jimmy the cash register. That's why. They made a stupid kid's mistake."

"Why'd you do that?" Rosie asked. She looked first at Rollie and then at Tommy, both of whom sat, tight-lipped.

"They wanted a moped." Mrs. Hackman sighed.

I changed the subject. "Rollie, you were down at the beach when Clement arrived that day—the day they found the stuff from the cryobank. I guess you're down there a lot?"

His mother answered for him. "He goes out to the beach a lot of mornings. To draw."

"Is that right?" I asked, addressing myself to the boy again. He nodded. "Did you look at it at all? What did you think it was?"

Tommy snorted, looking sideways at his brother, who stuck his chin out at me and kept his eyes as far from Rosie as he could.

"I thought it was a bunch of junk. Chief Paisley wouldn't say anything when I asked him why he was messing with it." Though Tommy seemed amused, his older brother still looked sullen. I was beginning to wonder how such a depressed kid could produce work with so much space and light in it. Maybe, I thought, the beach was the one thing that made him happy.

"You saw it there, then you saw the chief . . . did you see anything else earlier? Anyone else?"

"No," he said softly.

"Are you sure, son?" Mrs. Hackman asked.

"Mom!" he protested.

"Okay," she said. "The boy says he didn't see anything."

"So," I said. "You guys didn't do it. Who do you think did?"

Tommy spoke up. "Perry. He's stupid enough to do something like that."

"Hey," Hackman said, "don't talk that way about a policeman."

"He's dumb."

"And he caught you jimmying the cash register at Frank's, so I guess he ain't all that stupid, right?" Hackman yelled. Tommy set his lips again. I guessed he wouldn't say another word.

"I think that old Hilda," Rollie said. I was glad he had decided to say something. "She's always talking about how bad the place is."

"Hilda?"

"She's related to little Joanne? Fredda Carey? You know them," Mrs. Hackman elaborated.

I nodded. "You mentioned her, too, I remember. And Perry."

Her husband looked disgusted. "She don't like Perry because he's my buddy. You can scratch that." He glared at her and she glared back at him.

"Buddy!" Mrs. Hackman said. "Drinking buddy, anyway."

"But Hilda must be pretty old if she's Joanne's great-aunt," Rosie said.

"I don't know how she did it," Mrs. Hackman said stubbornly. "Maybe she had an accomplice. Like Frank."

"You also mentioned Wolf," Rosie continued. "What made you think of him?"

"Well, think about it. He used to go with Nora and she walked out on him. And look what happened to his girlfriend. Something's wrong with that man. I never trusted him. I think he's got it in for the whole female sex."

"And you've got it in for my friends," Hackman groused. "Wolf's a good man."

Rosie cut in. "Were he and Gracie having problems?"

"I heard they argued sometimes," Mrs. Hackman said.

"Oh, hell," Hackman said. "Everybody argues."

"You and your pals." She sighed.

We stayed for a bit longer, but the conversation kept going in circles, and it didn't look like the Hackmans were going to be much help that night. About all we'd gotten out of the visit was a slightly reinforced suspicion of Wolf, who we already knew was unaccounted for, so far, when Gracie hit the rocks.

And a funny feeling that Rollie might be hiding something.

My shoulder was giving me trouble, and I felt tired and angry and frustrated. I signaled to Rosie, we thanked our hosts, and started back to the motel.

Joanne was no longer sitting on her front porch. The street was quiet. Television voices nattered from a couple of houses, living room lights were on. But the night was chilly and no one was outside.

Even on Main Street nothing much was happening. Music from the tavern. Both restaurants mostly empty. I felt quiet too. The walk was working the kinks out of my mind, but I was having trouble thinking logically.

"What do you think of Rollie?" I asked.

"Strange kid, but Alice likes him. And the parents . . . God, what a depressing house."

I agreed. And I wondered how far Rollie could go with his talent, coming from that place. He'd have to be really determined, and he'd have to be smart enough to learn, on his own, how to live in the world that seemed to have battered his parents to death.

I said good night to Rosie, took a pill, and fell asleep.

— *18* —

We had a lot of work lined up for Monday. First on the list was a quick run to the spit to talk to a woman named Filomena Barth, the older woman who made her home there.

Clement had told Rosie she was, indeed, a poet. The second item of business was a stint at Nora's bank. Nora had reluctantly given us a small office and had promised to make a general announcement about us.

I had filled Rosie in on the things I had learned about the bank earlier, and she had decided there were a lot of gaps in our knowledge of the cryo-business. I wasn't sure we needed to know more. She was. She offered to go down to the bank and get things set up while I checked on the poet. I took her up on it.

Filomena Barth's house was the one I'd earlier classified as modest, next door to the one I'd classified as humble. It was a tidy brown shingle, the trim painted deep red, that looked like it had been picked off a side street in Berkeley and dropped beside the ocean. Hydrangeas clustered under the front windows. A Monterey pine, planted close to the house, sheltered its face.

Something rubbed against my leg, and I looked down. A perfectly petite and beautiful black cat, female in all her moves, was batting her eyelashes at me. She wore a red collar with a red tag that said "Sara." I knelt to pet her. As I was saying, "Hello, Sara," the door opened and a woman stepped out on the threshold. I stood quickly to introduce myself.

She had been just about to have a glass of beer, she said. Would I join her? I resisted the urge to look at my watch—I knew it was just after nine in the morning—and said I'd be delighted.

"Unless you'd like a toddy or something warming?"

"No, beer's fine."

"Yes, and good for you in the morning. Like cereal." She led me into a living room decorated in earth colors. A fire was burning in the brick fireplace, which needed tuckpointing badly.

I sat on a brown corduroy easy chair, she took the red one.

She was at least eighty years old, and wore her fine gray hair in a bun. She was dressed in a gypsy skirt and a yellow turtleneck sweater, and wore beaded moccasins on her feet. The rug, I noticed, was Navajo.

"I want to thank you for being so hospitable," I began, remembering Melody's evaluation of the woman as solitary and unfriendly.

She smiled. "I've heard about you and your friend, and I've been curious about you. I like the way you look, and the way you pet my cat."

"I have cats."

"I'm not surprised."

There was a silence during which we regarded each other warmly.

"You're a poet," I said.

"And you're a journalist."

"No, I'm not." She only raised her eyebrows. "I'm . . ." There it was again. What am I, anyway? Maybe I should just get a license, especially if there are going to be some people I can't lie to. "I'm investigating the break-in at the bank. The cryobank."

She laughed. "Do you think I have something to do with that? I assure you, menopause is long past."

"I'm also looking into Gracie Piedmont's death."

She nodded, sipping at her beer. "Would you like some pretzels?"

"No, thanks."

"And you're wondering if I know anything about what happened out here on Friday night?"

"Yes. Did you see anything? See her drive past? Anything that happened when she was here?"

She ate a pretzel. "No, I'm afraid not. I had put up my shutters that afternoon, and Sara and I were tucked up quietly by the fire when I heard all that commotion later— the police, the ambulance, and whatever else there was. I thought about going out to see what had happened, but to tell you the truth, I was working on a poem about the storm and I thought I would find out soon enough if it concerned me, and a little later if it didn't."

"Could you tell me who your neighbors are, on either side?"

"Inland is Frank Wooster." She gave me a sly, almost nasty look, and we both laughed. That was the house I kept thinking of as humble. Maybe it was a crooked house with a crooked man? "And on the other is that young couple. He was in business. Does something with money, still."

"So you saw nothing from—when did you put up your shutters?"

"Four or four-thirty, it must have been. I can't be more exact than that."

"And they were up until after the body was discovered?"

"They were up until the next day. You're not as tall as Magnum, but you're nearly as good-looking."

"Thank you."

"I'll be going away for a day or two. I have a daughter in Mill Valley. But I hope we'll meet again when I come back."

"I hope so too." I got the feeling I was expected to leave. Maybe she wanted to work on a poem. I got up, thanked her again, and left. I think I was a little bit in love.

I found Rosie in a room on the bank's second floor. She had barely gotten started, because Nora had not had a room waiting and there was much shifting around before Rosie could begin.

Most of the employees had little to do with the storage area. The front desk receptionist had nothing useful for us, Rosie reported, and most of the clerical staff dealt with more immediate matters. But we wanted attitudes as well as information. Were any of them disgruntled, angry, dissatisfied? It seemed to us that the act of destruction was more likely to be the work of someone who didn't get a raise than of a pair of kids or a religious groupie. Maybe someone who had been fired?

The personnel manager assured us that while several people had left in the last two years for one reason or another, no one had been, as she put it, "terminated." Why had various people left? Had any of them left angry? Any particular problems with anyone? She didn't think so, didn't remember anything specific. So, she said, nothing very terrible could have happened, or she'd remember.

"It might not have been terrible in your eyes, only in theirs," Rosie said.

She saw that there might be some sense in that. "Maybe I could go through my files and see if there's anything . . ." she said tentatively. "But I'm not sure when I could do that. Not today, certainly."

We managed to convince her that we really needed any information she might have, and soon, and after a lot of negotiating got her to promise she would work on it that evening. I think I charmed her.

The bank's medical consultant—Dr. Reid, her name was—was immune to my charm, but not to Rosie's.

Rosie had made a point of telling me that I hadn't found out much, in my first talk with Nora, about the women who were the bank's customers. The doctor was happy to fill us in.

"I know almost nothing about this process," Rosie began. "Is it safe?"

"We do everything we can to make it safe," Dr. Reid said. "One of the good things about freezing is that it gives us time to put the sperm in quarantine until it's been tested. The donors and their sperm go through very careful genetic and medical screening."

"Do you reject very many of them?"

"Yes. Some weeks as many as eighty percent."

"What about AIDS?" I asked.

"That's part of the medical screening of the sperm. The AIDS antibody test. It shows whether the donor has been exposed."

"Say I were going to do this," Rosie said. "How much would it cost? How would it be done? What are the rules?"

Dr. Reid smiled. "Rules?" They laughed. "We have a sliding scale, so your cost would depend on your income. Anywhere from five to fifteen hundred dollars, I believe, although that's not exactly my area of expertise." They smiled at each other again. "You would go through an orientation that would cover legal matters and donor screening, that kind of thing. Then there's a class on the fertility cycle, and of course you would get a complete physical." She paused.

"When do I pick my donor—or is it donors?"

The doctor laughed. "How many did you want? One donor at a time, please."

"All right," Rosie said agreeably. I was beginning to feel like I should be somewhere else.

"You'd go through the donor files and take your pick. There's consultation for that, too, of course."

I decided to get more involved in the conversation. "So she's picked her donor. Then what?"

The doctor took her eyes off Rosie long enough to smile at me. She was about my age, tall and slender, with medium length blond hair and bright blue eyes with laugh lines. She was tan, in January. I liked having her smile at me.

"Then we wait for her fertile time, and she makes an appointment for her insemination visit or pickup."

"Pickup?" Rosie asked.

"Some women use their own doctor. Some prefer to do it at home, themselves, or with the help of a friend."

I thought that sounded like fun, but I wouldn't have said so for anything in the world.

"What else do I get for my money?" Rosie asked.

"Pregnancy test. And six months worth of tries, if you need them."

"Six months?" I said. "How much do you get from one guy?"

"We buy insemination units in threes. But donors can repeat. And of course a woman can try an alternate donor."

There was a point here that was fascinating me. "Do you mean to say a guy could keep donating indefinitely and have maybe hundreds of kids born through this bank?"

"No. We limit each donor to ten live births."

So much for a strange fantasy. Then I remembered something Nora had told me about donors, and a question that had occurred to me later.

"Nora told me that some donors are men who are about to have vasectomies." She nodded, giving me her full attention. "In case they want to have kids later. But I've heard that a vasectomy can be reversed. So if you wanted . . ."

"Why go through another procedure when it can be stored? Also, reversals sometimes don't work and sometimes they're only temporary—scarring can cause obstruction again. Some doctors advise their male patients to store sperm immediately after a reversal, just in case."

I reflected that there were an awful lot of ways for a sperm bank to make money.

"I want to get back to this home insemination," Rosie said, and I lost the doctor again. "You just carry it home, thaw it out. . . ?"

"You take it home packed in dry ice, thaw it, and use it as soon as possible."

"It lives for only a day once it's thawed," I explained to Rosie.

"That's right. And it thaws in ten minutes at room temperature."

"What if you take it home, thaw it out, and then something happens and you can't use it right away?"

"You would have a problem, Rosie," the doctor said, laughing. "And I wouldn't advise tucking it in with the TV dinners. You'd kill it."

"But your kind of quick-freeze doesn't?"

"Some percentage of sperm die even when the method is very fast and very cold. All our sperm must first pass a freeze-tolerance test."

This was all very interesting, but we had a lot of people to talk to, and besides, I wanted lunch. I thanked the doctor, Rosie thanked the doctor, she said we were very welcome, indeed, and left. We went to get a sandwich and were back in half an hour.

We talked with several employees who dealt directly with donors or recipients. Despite orders from above to be open with us, they were all very nervous about confidentiality. Did any of them recall anyone who was particularly dissatisfied with services or product? They were all shocked at the question, and most of them said no such thing had ever happened. One woman did remember a couple of prospective clients who had read all the donor profiles and declared themselves to be dissatisfied with the possibilities, but they had been given their money back.

"About those possibilities," Rosie said. "I guess you have a pretty broad spectrum of donors?"

"Oh, yes."

"What kind of spectrum? I mean in terms of what?"

"Oh, education, interests, health history, occupation, ethnic background."

"And every woman gets to see information about every donor?"

"About every donor whose sperm is available. There are no profiles on the private storage people, of course."

"And mostly women can find what they want?"

"Certainly. Some people are just unbelievably picky."

I asked her if she by any chance remembered who these dissatisfied prospects were.

There was one from Marin County, she said, and one who had come all the way from Santa Cruz. But neither of them had been really angry. Anyone local? Well, yes, as a matter of fact. Gracie Piedmont had stopped in once during her lunch break—there was no rule against employees using the service, she assured us—and looked through the donor profiles.

"She said she was just curious, but who knows? Anyway, she looked, but she didn't find what she wanted, I guess, because she never followed up on it. I mean, she didn't complain or anything, if that's what you're after. And you have to understand, that was a favor to her, as a fellow employee. You know, I mean, no one can just walk in here off the street, not pay anything, and check out the profiles to see what they can see."

"Absolutely not," I said.

We talked to a few more people before we got to the one who, with Nora, had access to all the confidential files and to the tank room, the one who had come in just after Nora the morning after the burglary.

"What a mess that was," she said.

"A mess?" Rosie asked. "I thought they just broke in, took the stuff, and took it to the beach."

"Well, that, yes. But someone got into the files too. Pried them right open, got them all mixed up. It took days to put them right."

"Pried?" I groaned. "I didn't see any pry marks on the cabinets."

"Of course you didn't." She was indignant. "By then we'd put everything in new ones. You can't keep confidential files in cabinets with broken locks. In fact, we had that done in a few hours, just put all the messed-up files in the new drawers and worked from there."

"Great work," I said.

"I guess Clement thought that was just part of the prank," Rosie said to no one in particular.

"I don't know. I didn't talk to Clement. Perry was the one who came out when we first called."

So, after several hours work, we came up with two interesting bits of information. The dead woman had been thinking of becoming a client at her own company, and the files had been rifled. I wanted to talk to Fredda again about her cousin and I wanted to know more about what had happened to those files. Would kids have broken into them? Maybe, for a laugh, to see what kind of men would want to be donors. The two who were under suspicion were, after all, budding men themselves. Natural curiosity? Part of the joke? I called Nora on the intercom and checked with her. Yes, she said, the files had also been broken into—was that significant?

"Did Clement know about it?"

"I suppose he did. I think he must have. He came out later, after he went with Perry to the beach, and looked around."

"Had the cabinets been replaced by then?"

"No, that was later in the day."

Rosie and I went to talk to Clement. He was sitting behind his desk, reading some reports, and waved us in happily, shoving the papers aside.

I got right to it. "Clement, why didn't you say anything about the bank donor files—the confidential files—being messed with?"

"Oh, hell, Jake, I don't think that's important."

"Why not? Whoever was there would have had to hang around for a while. Wouldn't kids be too scared to do that? Why would religious fanatics look at the files? Why not destroy them, if anything?"

Clement leaned back in his swivel chair, put his feet up on the desk. "Okay. You got me. Can I trust you not to make a damned fool of me in print?"

"Yes, absolutely." No lie. There wouldn't be any print unless *Probe* actually did decide to do a piece, and I thought I might be able to protect Clement even so.

"It was that damned asshole"—he glanced at Rosie—"Perry. Maybe he was hung over. He screwed up bad. He took the call. He saw the files and the freezers. He told them not to touch the freezers or the window but he didn't say anything about the files. By the time I got over there later there was a woman working away at those cabinets, taking the files out, smearing her hands all over everything. If there ever was anything to see, anything at all, there wasn't anymore."

"No prints?"

"Drawers were all smudged up. Folders too. And there must have been a thousand of those. We found a couple of her prints, clean, but that was it. And there wasn't anything on the freezers. But I don't see what difference it makes to you. Same story. Break-in, vandalism."

"It could make a big difference," I said.

He swung his feet to the floor. "Okay. But a man my age can't afford to make too many mistakes. Oh, nobody's going to take away my pension, but I'm not ready to leave this job yet. To tell you the truth, it keeps me company."

"You didn't make the mistake," Rosie objected. "Perry did."

"Same thing, in the end, Rosie. I'm responsible for this town."

"Is that the only thing you haven't told us?"

He nodded. "It's not like I'm keeping a lot of secrets here, Jake. It didn't seem to matter, early on. I figured it was just those two kids who did it, anyway, the Hackmans. Can't you picture a couple of bright boys getting a kick out of reading those files?"

I could, but I wasn't ready to. "You still think that?"

"A lot of different things have happened. The bank. Gracie. Your truck. There's not a lot of doubt in my mind that someone tampered with your brakes. That's no innocent kid's prank. We've got something serious going on here."

"So you're willing to concede that now?"

He stared at me, coldly. "Damn it, Jake, let's not talk about conceding, okay? Perry messed up. I messed up. But I don't know what's connected to what and neither do you."

That was true. And I wondered, for just a second, whether it might not be better to admit we weren't reporters after all if Clement was worried about his mistakes being made public. But much as I liked the man, he represented the law, so I let the thought die. I told him what we'd learned about Gracie Piedmont looking through the donor profiles. He understood that was the public part of the donor files, the part the customers got to see.

"What's next for you?" he asked.

"We came here to find out about the break-in, and that's the angle we're going to take for the time being. But Gracie's death keeps coming up. There's a connection. What about you?"

He ran down a list of all the people he'd talked to. The only one he'd seen so far that we hadn't was Great-aunt Hilda, a treat I'd been saving. "I haven't come up with a damned thing worth using."

"Neither have we," I admitted. "Yet."

—19—

Frank Wooster was sunning himself, an old wooden kitchen chair tilted against the warped boards of his garage. The truck looked the same as it had the day before.

He nodded at us, but he didn't move.

"Any news on the truck?" Rosie asked.

"New axle's on the way. Body man's coming in tomorrow, like I already told you. But we got a problem."

"What's that?"

"Can't seem to track down a new fender. Not much we

can do with that one." He jerked his greasy gray head toward the interior.

"What can you do, then?"

He shrugged. "I'll make a couple more calls, but I got a feeling it'll be easier for you to find junk parts down around San Francisco. Lots of junk down there." He didn't quite sneer. I wanted to punch him out, but I didn't think that would be a great idea.

We walked the half mile to Fredda Carey's house. Besides Wolf, she seemed to be the only person who might know why Gracie Piedmont had been interested in the donor profiles. Fredda answered the door, and there was no sight or sound of the wheelchair. Joanne, I guessed, was at school.

"Well, hello again," she said. "I don't know how I'm supposed to get any work done with people coming around to ask me things all the time." She added nervously, "That's a nice dog. Does he bite?"

"No, she doesn't," Rosie said.

"We understand that you're busy," I assured her. "But we do have a question about Gracie. . . ." She shrugged, sighed, and waved us inside.

Rosie told Alice to stay on the porch, since, despite her assurance that the dog was not vicious, Fredda clearly did not trust the animal.

Once again she invited us to join her in the kitchen while she worked. Once again we watched her circular movement from oven to refrigerator to table to freezer to table as she operated her system.

Rosie began the conversation on a social note, mentioning that we had, the day before, visited Nora's folks in their neat little house.

"Nice people," she said. "Very nice people. It's wonderful how they've got Nora to see to things for them, so they can have a pretty home and a comfortable old age." She sighed again, gazing around her kitchen. "Some of us have to put enough by on our own." She cut circles of dough and lined them up, soldierlike, on a cookie sheet. "That Nora is some kind of go-getter. I've got a lot of admiration for that woman. Real brainy. You got to be smart to make it in this world."

"What we actually came to talk to you about," I said, "was something we heard at the sperm bank this morning. Something about your cousin."

She took one cookie sheet out of the oven, put the new one in, put the finished ones on top of the refrigerator, took the cooled ones down from the refrigerator and dumped them in bags, took the bags to the freezer, which didn't look as full as it had the last time we'd seen it. "What about Gracie?"

"That she was interested in maybe using the bank's services, that she read through all the profiles of the donors but didn't take it any further."

Fredda looked thoughtful. "She could have." She flattened another ball of dough. "I guess she did, if someone says she did."

"But why would she? Was there some problem with Wolf?"

She laughed. "Now, how would I know that?"

"We heard he'd had a child with his first wife," Rosie said. "Unless something has happened to him since then . . ."

Fredda gave us her shrug. "Not that I've heard."

"But she was planning on marrying him?"

"I guess so. Listen, who knows anything about anybody else? Maybe that was before she decided to marry him. Or maybe she was changing her mind and wasn't ready to say so. Or maybe she was just bored and felt like reading something. I couldn't say."

"So you don't know any reason why she might have been looking for a donor?" Rosie persisted. "You don't remember her saying anything? And you don't know whether Wolf can still father children? She really never talked to you about any of that?"

Fredda got slightly irritated. "Not that I remember. But she could have said something and I just forgot. I'm a busy woman, you know. I can barely keep up with my own problems." She was cutting out those damned little circles again.

We thanked her and asked her the way to Great-aunt Hilda's house. I felt like Little Red Riding Hood.

"What do you want with her?" She stared at us.

"Nothing much," Rosie replied.

On our way down the street Rosie smiled. "She didn't offer us any cookies this time. Alice would have loved one."

The directions took us a couple of blocks north and east— away from the ocean and away from downtown. The street looked slightly less poor than Fredda's, but this house, too, was nearly paint-bare.

Great-aunt Hilda was on the front porch holding a wet string mop when we strolled up the walk. I don't know what I had expected. A female version of Frank Wooster, maybe. But this woman was no lean, ascetic Bible-belt-style crank. She was a big, fat, sloppy California crank.

She must have topped two-fifty. Her hair was combed straight down all the way around in a short Buster Brown. She looked to be around sixty, but who could tell.

She wore one of those print housedresses that no one wears anymore, with big brown flowers on it. She had little blue eyes in a round, lumpy face. She put a large, puffy hand on the sagging rail and frowned at us.

"Hi," I said.

I don't like to judge people by appearances, even people with mean eyes in big faces with broken blood vessels in the cheeks. Even when they frown at my friendly greeting. After all, some people are nearsighted.

We walked to the foot of the porch steps. She pointed the mop head at us.

"You must be those reporters from San Francisco," she said. "I don't know what you want with me, but I'm busy.

I'm washing the kitchen floor now." She turned and lumbered toward the open front door.

"Please," I said. "If we could just have a word or two with you."

She looked at our shoes, and she looked at the dog, none of which appeared to pass inspection. "Wait out here while I finish the floor." I didn't think she'd let us near her clean floor. I wasn't even sure she'd come back out again.

She did come back, in about five minutes, by which time we had moved up the stairs and onto the porch, which displeased her. We began to cross the boards to get within conversational distance.

"Don't come any closer."

"We don't mean you any harm," Rosie said, "and the dog is gentle. We just want to talk."

"It's not the dog I'm worried about, and you're close enough." We were about five feet away from her.

"All right," I said. "We've been talking to your niece about some of the things that have happened in town lately, and we wanted to get your feelings about them. About the break-in a couple of weeks ago, and about Gracie Piedmont's death. How were you related to Gracie, anyway?"

"Indirectly," she said.

"We're asking people in town why they think someone might have wanted to vandalize the bank," Rosie said, deciding, apparently, to veer away from Gracie for a moment.

I leaned against a porch railing, and she looked at me as if I'd lifted my leg on it, dog fashion. My shoulder hurt and was making me tired. I kept leaning.

"How would I know? Filthy place. I can't imagine why anyone would want to go near it. I never could guess why that Gracie wanted to work there, or why Fredda would want to associate with anyone who did. Spreading disease, that's what I say."

"Disease?" I asked.

"You live in San Francisco," she barked. "You know perfectly well what I'm talking about. Disease. Death."

"I see," I said. "Then you must be upset that the thieves threw what they stole into the ocean. Spreading disease."

She nodded slowly. "I told my little Joanne not to go near that beach for six months."

"Do you think the people who committed the vandalism were infected?" Rosie asked.

"I wouldn't be surprised. Crazy."

"But the note they left said they did it to fight ungodly wickedness," Rosie said. "Don't you think that's a good reason?"

She snorted, glaring at Rosie. "Young lady, don't try to make me think you think so."

"What about Nora, then?" I asked. "Do you feel she's doing something evil?"

"I won't argue religion with you, young man."

"But how do you feel about her? She's doing so much good with her money, taking care of her family. That's virtuous, isn't it?"

"Some people don't care where their money comes from. And I'll tell you this, if Fredda tried to help me with that kind of filth, I wouldn't accept it. I'll tell you what seems wicked to me. That Nora can take care of her family and Fredda can't. Because Joanne and me could use some money. If it was clean money. Oh, Fredda scrapes along. She makes do. No fancy gardeners or house painters, like some people. Fredda had to learn to do everything for herself because that's what you do when you're poor. It's a dirty shame." She shook her large head and her wattles quivered.

"That is too bad," I said. "I'm sure Joanne has a lot of needs that money could help with."

"Oh, yes. But the sins of the mother . . ."

"Were you at all close to Gracie?" Rosie asked.

"Not anymore."

"You know why she went out to the spit the night she died, don't you?" I asked.

She nodded. "To see if that house was all right, that's what I heard. That Mr. Segal's house."

"Spiegel. And she slipped and fell, or got washed off the scarp—you knew that?"

"I don't know how she fell. The kind of life she led, maybe she was drunk. Or maybe that boyfriend of hers pushed her. Men get tired of the cow when they don't have to pay for the milk."

I was stopped by that, for just a minute, and caught myself trying to get at her logic until I got back on the track.

"You think her boyfriend killed her?" Rosie wanted to know.

"I don't think anything. I don't know anything about people like that. It's all I can do just to try to keep Joanne from seeing too much in this town, the way things are going these days. To keep her following the word, obeying the Bible."

"Doesn't her mother take care of that?"

She shook her head. "She wouldn't know how." She turned halfway away from us, preparing to go back inside. "I have to take care of my house now. The child's coming today."

"You're very close to Joanne, aren't you?" I asked.

She turned that heavy face toward me one more time. A heavy, angry, sad face. "The child came into this world with a heavy burden. I'm doing all I can to save her soul."

At that moment Frank Wooster came walking up to the house. Astoundingly, he was carrying a little bouquet of flowers.

"The child's coming in a while, Frank," she told him.

He grunted disgustedly. "Then I won't stay long."

He glared at us, and the two of them went into the house together and closed the door.

—20—

Dinner seemed like a good idea, but I wanted to talk about the case in some detail and I didn't think it would be easy to do that in a public place, with the whole damned town listening, directly or indirectly, to the two "reporters from San Francisco."

We picked up burgers and fries at Georgia's and took them back to the motel. Long after the food was gone we were still going around in circles, trying to make some sense of the crime rampage we seemed to be involved in.

Rosie wrote out a list of suspects under three headings: vandalism, murder (?), and truck crash. We were hoping to see some cross-category likelihoods.

The first point to be decided, though, was what to call the attack on the bank. Was it vandalism? Now that we knew the thief had gone through the files, or at least rummaged around in them, we had to reconsider the cause. Maybe someone was after information? Maybe some files had been stolen and no one was aware of it yet? Maybe most of the sperm—it was valuable, after all—had actually been stolen? We stuck a question mark after the word *vandalism* to go with the one after the word *murder*.

Under the first heading, then, we listed Frank Wooster, Aunt Hilda, and Joanne. Now that I'd seen Aunt Hilda, I could imagine her doing almost anything. She didn't move well or quickly, but she looked strong enough to lift crates of rocks in the service of the Lord. On general principles we added Wolf to the list, because he was Nora's ex-boyfriend if for no other reason. Then came the Hackmans, followed by generic disgruntled employee and generic disgruntled client.

As an afterthought I added disgruntled donor. Maybe some-one who had been rejected? Rosie was dubious about that.

"You mean someone might have thought the bank was im-pugning his manhood?"

"Sure." The more I thought about it, the better I liked it. Next came murder (?), which I wanted to change to "death."

"If it wasn't murder," Rosie said reasonably, "there's no point in talking about it."

That made sense, I had to agree, so for the sake of our deliberations, we would consider it murder. This second list was harder than the first. We decided to include several peo-ple who were involved in the events of that night one way or another. Perry, who had found the body. Wolf.

"What about the guy who asked her to go out there in the first place?" Rosie wanted to know. I argued that he hadn't exactly asked her, or said he hadn't, and that he was in L.A. at the time. But since we had no proof in either case, we added Marty Spiegel. Fredda, because she had been with the dead woman that evening. And all the other residents of the spit who were actually living there at the time. Which in-cluded Henry Linton and Frank Wooster.

That took us to the truck crash. Whoever removed those nuts knew at least a little bit about cars. We had seen Wooster at the garage before we'd driven to the beach, and he'd driven the wrecker out after the crash. Could he have been on the road in the interim?

"Don't forget the Hackman kids' father seems to be work-ing on that car in the yard," Rosie said. Possibly he was. I suspected half the people in town knew enough about cars to lose the brake fluid, if it came to that, but we had to start with what we knew. We added Melody Clift, because we had actually seen her in the area, and, again, Spiegel, be-cause he was on the road soon after the crash.

The category-crossers, those who qualified easily as suspects in at least two categories, were Wolf, Marty, the Hackmans, and Frank Wooster.

We drew up another list. People to see or find out about. Where was Wolf at the time Gracie died? Check on it. The residents of the spit—what were their connections with the bank or with Gracie? Was Spiegel really in L.A. that night or had he called from someplace closer? How did Frank Wooster feel about getting germs from the bank's assets? Did he have a connection with Gracie we hadn't yet discovered?

We still needed to get information about unhappy bank employees, who would also, after all, have known Gracie.

"How long has the bank been there?" Rosie asked. I realized I didn't know. "Because we do know one person who would be an unhappy client if she had been a client." She peered at me, waiting for me to catch up with her. I was there already.

"Fredda. Her kid was born disabled. A birth defect. There doesn't seem to have been a husband. You're saying, what if the birth came about as a result of the bank? And Fredda's bitter about it?"

"Or Hilda."

"The kid's twelve years old. Kind of a long wait for revenge."

Rosie stretched out on the bed and stared at the ceiling thoughtfully. "Maybe there was never the right opportunity before."

"And how would Gracie come into it?"

"They're related. She could have been involved somehow. She and Fredda were friends."

"And for some reason Gracie was interested in the donor files."

So there was a fourth list. Information we still needed to get to fill in the gaps in the lines we were following.

The three unanswered questions that interested me the most at the moment were Wolf's whereabouts at the time of the death at the spit, any reason Fredda might have for a grudge against the bank, and, my favorite and mine alone, the insulted donor.

—21—

I woke up the next morning around nine, thinking about doing something that had nothing to do with the case, or not much, anyway. I wanted to visit Louis's gallery and take a better look at Rollie Hackman's work. Off and on, the day before, I had thought about the boy, and his family, and I had decided to buy something. What the hell, it was a good investment.

Lou Overman was reading a paperback. He looked up when Rosie and I walked in.

"I hope you haven't come to ask me—again—what I heard or saw on the night of the burglary. Nothing. Nothing. Nothing. Satisfied?"

"We came to buy something," I told him.

"Oh?" He wasn't impressed.

"Something by Rollie Hackman."

"Oh!" He looked pleased.

I deliberated for a long time before I decided. I liked a watercolor of Main Street, with the tavern and the drugstore foremost, but I was particularly attracted to the drawings of the beach, debris-strewn and deserted. Rosie made up her mind quickly, as she often does, and bought a charcoal sketch of the spit, seen from a distance along the beach, for fifteen dollars. I finally settled on a watercolor of the tri-angular rock formation offshore, where the vials of sperm had been dumped. It would be nice, I thought wryly, to have a memento. And there were no drawings of the bank itself.

We brought our purchases to the counter, and Lou approved.

"I think those are two of his best. Kid's got a future. At least I hope he does."

"What do you mean, hope?" I asked. "He's talented. He seems to have drive. Does a lot of work. Why shouldn't he succeed?" I had several ideas as to why he might not, like lousy genes, but those ideas pissed me off and made me want to argue.

"Talent, even with drive, isn't always enough," he sighed. "Sometimes things happen to people. They sink. Fade."

"Or make bad mistakes," Rosie said. "Like breaking into places."

He glared at her. "This conversation is getting unpleasant."

The bell over the door tinkled, and Joanne wheeled in. She was wearing a jacket that looked too big for her, and her lank hair needed combing. I wondered why she wasn't at school. She said hello to us without smiling, and nodded to Lou. Then she aimed for a rack of lurid paperbacks, on which I had noticed, earlier, a couple of Melody's books. I had thought about buying one. After all, I knew the author. But I couldn't bring myself to do it.

I was curious to see what the child had in mind. I didn't think Great-aunt Hilda would be too thrilled to see her there. While Lou was wrapping the painting and drawing, I wandered casually in her direction.

She was thumbing through something called *Forever Eden* by Melody Clift. I wondered whether there were any white fur rugs in it. I also wondered whether she'd written one called *Gone with the Breeze*.

When Joanne realized I had noticed what she was doing, she turned abruptly, glared at me with scared black eyes, and stuck the book back in the rack. She looked like Lou had looked a moment before when Rosie had made the crack about "breaking into places." Very much like he had looked.

I glanced back at him tying string around my package. The same thin face, the same eyes. The hair was different, but that look of anger was exactly the same.

I wondered if anyone else had ever noticed. I wondered if Joanne had.

"I wasn't actually reading it," she said.

"Would your mother be upset with you if you were?" I wasn't exactly wild about Fredda, but I felt compelled to act as if her mother, not her great-aunt, were the authority in her life.

"He shouldn't sell books like this," she said, and wheeled off to a table piled with books about northern California ecosystems. I pursued her.

She fiddled with the books.

"No school today?" I asked.

"I don't feel good."

"Sorry to hear it."

She wheeled away from me, up to the counter. I heard her telling Lou her mother needed a couple of boxes for delivering cookies. He went into the back room, got two book cartons, placed one inside the other, and set them on her lap. She wheeled out without another word to anyone.

Rosie and I took our packages and left. Walking back to the motel, I mentioned what I was thinking.

"You're right. There is a resemblance. She doesn't look exactly like him, though."

"You didn't catch the expression on her face when she realized I was watching her look at one of Melody's books. I felt like I was looking at Lou, not Joanne."

"Go on. I'm listening."

"Lou has strong connections with both Joanne and Rollie. He thinks a lot of Rollie, seems to really care about him. And he could have witnessed the burglary. I wonder if there's any connection between Rollie and Joanne, or Rollie and Hilda? Jesus, what a can of worms."

"Everybody's connected to everyone else," she groused. "The whole town probably has a common ancestor."

"Yeah. A Kallikak or a Juke. I want to add Overman to the list of cryobank suspects. For a lot of reasons. He could have seen something. And maybe he's a rejected donor."

"You mean something's wrong with him and that's why Joanne was born that way—there are a lot of reasons for birth defects, I think."

"Let's just check it out, anyway."

Since we didn't want to talk to or see Mrs. Hackman, we went to Georgia's for breakfast. Seated in a booth at the back were Henry and Wolf, Wolf with his back to the door. Henry nodded at us, and Wolf turned around. He stood up and came to our table.

"I hear you were looking for me yesterday," he said to Rosie.

She thought fast. "Not exactly. I just wanted to try to make peace with you. You were so angry at us the other day. No hard feelings, that kind of thing."

He sat down. "Sure. That's why you wanted to know if I was at work when Gracie died."

Henry stood up and came over too. "Wolf, why don't you let these people eat their breakfasts?" He stopped, gazed at us benignly. "Better yet, why don't you two join us in that back booth. Let's have a talk. Clear the air."

I was tempted to ask, "What's it to you?" There was something about his manner that offended me. Big Daddy making peace among his children. But my investigative side shut me up. We joined them.

The waitress brought coffee and took our orders. Henry got back to his soft scrambled eggs, sausage, and whole wheat toast. Wolf let his sit and congeal.

"This man," Henry said, tilting his head toward Wolf, "has been through hell in the past few days."

We waited, silent.

"His fiancée was killed in a terrible accident. You were there in the bar when I came in to tell him. You saw how he was."

I nodded. "But if it wasn't an accident? He wasn't working when it happened, he was working after she was found."

Our food arrived. "Maybe Wolf can tell us," I continued, "where he was between five and six o'clock?"

"I don't know why I should tell you anything. I told Clement. He asked me this morning and I told him. And I'm sick and tired of people looking at me funny because you two are asking questions. Because your questions are making people wonder."

"Then why don't you tell us too," Rosie said. "We could ask Clement. We'd rather hear it from you."

"Who the hell do you think you are, anyway? I thought you were here to find out about that business over at the bank. Why all this shit about Gracie?" I was startled to see a couple of big tears spill over his lower lids. He wiped them away.

"Wolf," Henry said, "maybe they think there's a connection. Because you used to go with Nora."

Wolf stared at us, dumbfounded. "That was years ago for Christ's sake." I shrugged. He turned to Henry. "You think these people have any right to be going around asking questions about me?"

Henry shook his head. "No, I don't. But it might be a good idea to do what you can to get them off your tail, you dumb shit."

Wolf's shoulders slumped. He pushed his plate into the center of the table, nearly tipping over my coffee. "Ask Clement," he said. "He's probably already checked it out. I was over visiting Hackman. Having a sandwich and a beer with Howard. Gracie was eating with her cousin, so Howard said come on over for a bite. His wife was working the dinner shift, and his kids were getting dinner at the restaurant."

We finished our breakfasts fast. Mine, I thought, was going to sit like lead in the pit of my stomach. We went to see Clement.

"We hear Wolf's got an alibi for Friday night," I said.

He nodded. "News does get around, doesn't it? I was just talking to Hackman. Wolf was with him, he says. No reason to think he's lying."

I told him we'd been at the Hackman place the night before. That Mrs. Hackman had accused Wolf and Hackman, although he'd disagreed, hadn't said anything about being with Wolf that evening.

Clement laughed. "Hackman didn't know when any of it happened. Didn't know the hour. Didn't make a connection until I questioned him."

"Doesn't that seem strange?" Rosie asked.

"Not really. The man drinks. He doesn't keep track of things too good anymore."

I sat down on the hard bench under the window. I was unconvinced. "Then maybe he got his nights mixed up too?"

"I don't think so. Vonnie—that's his wife—she only works the dinner hour on Fridays. He can probably keep that straight enough. If he doesn't go over to the restaurant with the kids, he fends for himself. So unless he's lying, Wolf's probably clear."

There was also crime number three to consider—the truck sabotage. "What about Saturday?" I persisted. "Do we know Wolf was at the bar all afternoon? Maybe he was on the coast road and decided to give us a free brake job."

"Those are his hours. We can check on it."

"And what about Frank Wooster?" Rosie wanted to know. "Was the garage open all afternoon? Was he there?"

"He was there when I called for the wrecker. In fact, he was working on Henry's car, and I had to drag him away."

That didn't tell us much. The mechanic could have done the work on the truck and cut back to town in plenty of time to answer the garage phone.

As much as I wanted the truck-wrecker, though, it seemed pretty clear that for the moment the way to that crime was through the first two—the burglary and the murder.

—**22**—

We made a return visit to the bank.

The personnel director told us she'd spent hours the night before looking through the files, and she was sorry, but she hadn't been able to come up with any former or current employees who were obviously unhappy. No one had left, she said, "under a black cloud." No one had ever complained that the raise and promotion system was unfair.

"But I do have a theory," she said brightly. We were desperate enough to listen. "What if it was Gracie? She seemed kind of upset around here the last few days before she fell. And she looked through the profiles that time and never said anything about it again. Maybe she had some problem? And went off the deep end? And broke in here and took everything and then killed herself?"

"An interesting idea," Rosie commented generously. "Incidentally, when was it exactly that she looked at the donor profiles?"

"Oh, just a couple of weeks ago."

Against the woman's will we kept her for nearly another hour, questioning and questioning again her assertion that no one in the history of the bank had ever been unhappy, trying to learn more about Gracie. The time was wasted. According to her, everything was for the best in this best of all possible cryobanks.

We went to find Nora. She kept us waiting for half an hour before she agreed to let us take her away for lunch. We convinced her to take enough time to drive up to Rosewood with us, because I, for one, was getting tired of having my meals spoiled by indignant citizens.

She recommended an Italian place that she said was pretty good, which was not much of a recommendation. I was even less impressed when I saw that Fredda's all-natural cookies were listed with the desserts. We settled down with our plates of pasta. They turned out to be, after all, pretty good.

Nora agreed with her personnel director. No unhappy employees or ex-employees.

"Not in the whole history of the bank?" Rosie asked.

"And no really unhappy clients either?" I added.

Not that she knew of.

"How long has the bank been in existence?"

"Six years." So much for Joanne. She was twelve. If she was Lou Overman's child, it was by the usual method, which pretty much took care of the possibility that Fredda had a birth-defects grudge against the bank.

"There's something I've been wondering about," I said, changing the subject. "The sperm that was stolen was worth a lot of money, right?" She nodded. "And you can't be sure that all of it was dumped, right?" She nodded again. "What about this then—say someone dumped only some of it and stole the rest to sell? Would there be a market?"

Nora cut a ravioli in half, stuck in her fork, moved it back and forth in the sauce for a while. "That seems pretty unlikely, all in all. First, why wouldn't a thief steal all of it?" She ate the ravioli. "Second, I think it would be pretty hard to sell black market sperm without the facilities to back it up. People would be afraid of it. And it's not like the established banks are that difficult to use. And none of the files were stolen. How could anyone sell it without being able to give the client donor profiles to select from?"

"You could make up your own files," Rosie said.

"And who says the thief doesn't have a bank to sell out of?" I added.

"I'm afraid that's all pretty unlikely," Nora said. "The sperm was worth a great deal to us, but there would be no reason for another bank to steal it. It's not expensive or particularly hard to get. An interesting line of reasoning, but I'm afraid it doesn't make a lot of sense."

So that answered a couple of questions from our lists of the night before.

"About those donor files, Nora," I said, "we're going to have to go through them. This afternoon would be good." She started to object. "We have to. We can't help you otherwise." She shook her head, but it was in resignation. "Could you run down the system for us?"

She sipped her wine. "I'm beginning to be sorry I hired you. The vandalism was a big blow. Violation of confidentiality on top of that, could ruin us."

I commiserated. "I know how important that is, ethically, but at least two crimes and possibly a murder are involved here. On balance—"

"On balance," she snapped, "the point is not ethics. The point is loss of a business. My business. Ethics are a luxury. So is the social value of the bank. You buy them with money. Without money you can't have them or anything else."

Very eighties, I thought, but who was I to quibble? I was getting paid too.

"Okay," I shot back. "Since we're still working for you, how about cutting the crap and filling us in?"

She studied me for a moment, sipped more wine, looked at Rosie, who was not looking at her, nodded, and began. "You know the files are organized by number. Each container is numbered. A complete file includes all our information on the donor. Name, address, medical information, the agreement he signs giving up paternal rights. That kind of thing. It also includes a copy of the anonymous profile, which is the only part the prospective recipient sees. And of course there are different sets of numbers, depending on the category the donor falls into. Whether the sperm is being held for private use or is available."

"Say you were looking in the file," Rosie said. "How would you be able to tell which set of numbers was which?"

"They're organized by availability. The available ones are in their own drawers, labeled that way. The others are labeled by designated purpose. Under each of those headings is a set of numbered files. In each file is the information about the donor. You understand that only the available ones include the anonymous profile. Numbered. That's very important."

"The number is important?" Rosie asked.

"Well, yes. It identifies the donor in the future."

"You mean in case a recipient wants to use him again?"

"That, certainly, but also for the children."

"The children?" I didn't understand.

"Yes. The children. They get their father's numbers."

"I still don't get it. Why?"

"I would think that would be obvious." Nora was annoyed. "To avoid marriage to a sibling."

Ah-hah, I thought. That also explained, at least in part, why each donor was limited to ten live births. Twenty years or so down the road, it could be a real pain to keep falling in love with kin. A scenario rolled through my head: "I love you. What is your father's number? Oh, no, not again . . ."

"Were all the files broken into?" I asked.

"Yes."

"Tell me this. Your personnel director says Gracie seemed

upset the last few days before her death. Do you remember anything like that?"

A hard question for Nora. A several-ravioli question. "She did seem distracted."

"Do you have any idea whether the distraction might have started around the time of the break-in?"

"I think perhaps it did. She was upset by the crime. But then, we all were."

"Did she seem unusually upset?"

She sighed. "Possibly. It's hard for me to say. I'm afraid I'm not as observant as I should be. It does seem that she was more upset. I remember someone mentioned to me that she'd been talking to Gracie about some work or something and Gracie never heard a word the woman said."

"Nora," I finished off a meatball, "would anyone just off the street, so to speak, have known where to go to find those files and the tanks?"

"No, of course not. We didn't take clients in there. We had a separate file of profiles and we brought the profiles to them in another room. I suppose someone who had visited to see the profiles could, conceivably, have some idea. Somehow."

"But mostly it would be employees who would know exactly where to go?"

"Anyone familiar with the bank would know, but yes, that would be pretty much limited to employees."

"And possibly to nosy prospective clients?"

"Possibly."

"Then how would a couple of kids or a religious fanatic know where to go? Whoever broke in broke into the right room."

"They would know," she said, "if they could get an employee to tell them where to look."

"A good, order-following employee like Gracie?"

"I said she was a good employee. I never said she had a mind of her own."

Rosie eyed Nora coolly. "Even so," she said, her voice matching her look, "any employee could have told anyone."

Nora shrugged. I switched to something else that had been on my mind and asked her about Lou and Joanne.

"There has been some speculation, apparently," she said. "I wasn't in town when Joanne was born, but I have heard that Lou is probably the father."

"She looks like him," Rosie said.

"Oh, I don't know. I guess she might, a little." Nora finished her ravioli. "But what does that have to do with anything?"

"I don't know," I admitted. "But we're trying to get at this burglary, and I keep thinking it's odd that he heard and saw nothing that night. The burglars were around for a while. They broke the window. They must have had a flashlight. They messed around in the files and they moved the contents of your tanks through the window. They must have made some noise at some point. It would be handy if he had something to do with it."

"I still don't know what his being Joanne's father would have to do with the burglary." Nora was clearly impatient with this line of speculation.

"I don't either. But what I really want to find out is whether the files were rifled for fun or for information. Is Lou a donor?"

"I don't know."

"Is there some way to find out if he was ever rejected as a donor?"

"Yes. There's a file."

I was not looking forward to going back to the bank and spending the rest of the day looking through the donor files when I wasn't sure they would tell us anything. But that seemed to be a logical, if tedious, next step.

We drove back to Wheeler. Nora, with what looked like

relief, returned to her office. On our way to the file room, I glanced at Rosie, who had been quiet in the car.

"You're not exactly wild about Nora, are you?"

She laughed. "Oh, I don't really dislike her."

"She confuses me," I admitted. "One minute she's knifing a dead woman with her version of straight talk, and the next minute she's being polite about someone who doesn't admit he's got a kid."

"I don't think manners or morals come into it at all," Rosie said. "When she knows something—or thinks she does—she says what she knows. When she's unsure, she's uncomfortable, she gets bored. I think that's all there is."

"Oh, come on. You're saying this successful businesswoman is about as complicated as Alice."

"You're complicated, Jake. That's why she confuses you."

The woman in charge of the files confirmed what Nora had said. They were intact, nothing was missing. How did she know for sure? She knew, she said, because she had cross-index lists, whatever those were.

We made ourselves as comfortable as we could in the file room, and began a long afternoon of reading.

It was mildly interesting. A lot of different kinds of men with different backgrounds, talents, and occupations. We went through the availables first. Students made up the biggest group, as we'd been told, but there were laborers, businessmen, and professionals too. The profiles were an odd combination of personal information and cold description. Whoever wrote them could have been a botanist describing an intelligent tree. There was this one, for example:

Donor No. 340
Summary: Good intellectual and verbal ability, better than average looks, some musical talent.
Ancestry: Central European.
Occupation: Law student.

Born: 1960s.
Eye color: Blue.
Skin color: Fair.
Hair: Brown, curly, full.
Height: 1.8m (6'0")
Weight at 22 years: 77 kg. (170 lb.)
General appearance: Normal, average build, full face.
Personality: Strong presence, assertive, humorous, friendly.
Interests: Include reading, softball, bicycling, music.
Achievements: Law school scholarship, published in law review, first trumpet in college orchestra.
I.Q.: 150.
Art, creativity: Music mentioned above.
Athletics: High school baseball, no major achievements.
Manual dexterity: Good.
General health: Excellent.
Defects: Two grandparents developed duodenal ulcers, one in his forties, one in her fifties.
Blood type: O pos. Pressure: 120/75
Comment: Recurrence risk for ulcers estimated at 22 percent after age fifty.

What a guy. I hoped he wouldn't give up his trumpet when he was a successful, ulcer-ridden, aggressive lawyer.

I read through number 340's legal agreement with the bank, where he said he wouldn't come back whining for his paternal rights later on. I glanced at his medical records and various reports on his sperm. His surname sounded German. He had accepted what appeared to be the usual student payment for his donation—twenty-five dollars.

From the availables we moved on to men whose reasons

for being donors were part of their files, the guys in categories: the ones who were impregnating surrogates, the ones who had made arrangements with friends, the ones with medical reasons, and a very few who, for odds and ends of reasons, were saving it for posterity. Among the last was Marty Spiegel, donor number 126. If I'd felt like I was looking through keyholes before with the files of strangers, reading the file of an almost-friend, without his knowledge or consent, made me feel like one of those P.I.'s who takes pictures of unfaithful spouses. Sleazy. In his file, I discovered, was an agreement that should he die before his relationship with the bank had ended, his sperm would be turned over to the management of the executor of his estate, an attorney in L.A., who would then, I guessed, be charged with the responsibility of finding a suitable mother for his child. Or would he be directed to sprinkle it over the sea with Spiegel's ashes?

When we finished with the donors, we searched the lists of recipients. At the end of our reading we had come up with nothing much. None of the men we were thinking of as suspects, with the exception of Spiegel, was a donor. None of the women who were possibles was listed among the recipients.

Lou Overman was not a donor, past, present, or even rejected.

We stepped back out onto Main Street with our eyes and our tempers somewhat the worse for wear. I noticed a newspaper vending machine outside the drugstore full of hot-off-the-press *Wheeler Weekly*s, and bought one. I wondered whether the paper would have anything interesting to say about the excitement around town lately.

There was a sketchy article about the break-in at the bank, which must have been discovered after the deadline of the week before, and a story about Gracie Piedmont's death that treated it as an unfortunate accident during a bad storm.

Two paragraphs at the bottom of the front page mentioned another unfortunate accident—our crash on the coast road—and included the notation, at the end, to (see page 3).

Stopping long enough to turn to page three, I read on as I walked. The headline was "San Francisco Reporters on the Trail of Trouble." The story went downhill from there.

"Why are *Probe* magazine reporters Jake Samson and Rosie Vicente nosing around Wheeler?

"They're doing an article on the North Coast Cryobank, they say. We want to know what kind of story that would be? Why didn't *Probe* show any interest until the bank was broken into and vandalized by persons unknown? And why are they asking questions about the recent death of one of this town's citizens, who also happened to be an employee of the bank?

"What are they after? Why are they mercilessly harassing the recently bereaved?

"We're all friends and neighbors here in Wheeler, and maybe it's time someone told people from down around San Francisco that our town, our people, don't exist for their amusement, that our private sorrows have nothing to do with them, and that if anything untoward has actually happened here, we'll be the ones to set it right."

It went on like that for another couple of paragraphs, but I stopped reading and handed the paper to Rosie. She stopped in the middle of the sidewalk, read the piece through, then riffled some pages.

"Look," she said, pointing at the masthead. I looked. The publisher and editor was our friend Henry Linton, the mayor and patriarch of Wheeler.

—23—

Just as I got inside the door of my room someone knocked on it.

"Who's there?"

"Clement."

I let him in. "What's going on, Clement?"

"I just thought you might want to know about this. Rollie Hackman. His mom called me a couple of hours ago. Looks like he's run off."

"Run off?"

"Run away."

Suddenly I felt cold and scared, remembering Gracie, remembering our crash. "Are you sure he left on his own?"

Clement nodded. "That's what Tommy says. He says his brother told him he was leaving town for a while, that he'd get in touch, and tell the folks not to worry."

"What else does Tommy say?"

"Nothing. No matter what you ask him, he says he doesn't know the answer. I know that boy, Jake. If his brother said don't talk, he won't talk. Not even to his folks."

Maybe Tommy wasn't talking, and maybe the Hackmans didn't know anything, but there was one other place to go for information about Rollie, and that was Louis's gallery and bookstore. Clement went off on some mission of his own.

I banged on Rosie's door. No answer. I banged louder and heard a cry of rage from within. A minute later she came to the door, wrapped in her robe, dripping shower water on the floor.

Her disgust at being dragged out of the shower vanished when I told her about Rollie. In five minutes she was dressed and ready to go. We took Alice, who had been stuck in the motel during our hours at the bank, along with us.

Lou was just locking the door of the gallery from the inside when we arrived.

We made faces and yelled about how urgent our visit was. He shrugged and shook his head. He was closed. We yelled some more. He pointed to a door next to the big front window of the shop and jerked a thumb upward. An entrance to his apartment. The door was unlocked, and we got upstairs fast enough so that we had to wait a few seconds before his apartment door opened.

"What is it you want?" he asked in a neutral voice.

"Rollie's run away. What do you know about it?"

He sagged, and closed his eyes.

"That's terrible," he whispered. Then he regained his composure, stood up straight, and met my eyes. "What makes you think I know anything about it?"

I wanted to say "Your reaction to the news," but that wouldn't have been the right approach. Instead, I asked if we could come in and sit down.

"I don't see why you should. I don't know anything about this. It's awful."

He did look pretty unhappy, all right. Rosie and I walked in and sat down without an invitation.

"You like the kid," I said. "You sell his work and you're happy when someone else appreciates it. You're probably the only person in this town he can talk to about art. I don't think his parents are too helpful. Maybe he even thinks of you as some kind of mentor."

"I suppose he does."

"Anything more than that?"

He looked puzzled for a moment, then glared at me. "I'm not a pedophile, Samson. And in any case, I'm completely heterosexual." He glanced at Rosie. "No offense meant."

"None taken." She smiled.

"It's just that you seem to have other unacknowledged relationships," I said, "and I thought this might be one too."

His eyes went dead. "I don't know what you mean."

"Skip it for now. All I'm saying is that Rollie might have confided in you, something that would be helpful in finding him. I want you to think hard about anything he might have said lately, anything that might give us a clue. And while you're thinking, could I use your bathroom?"

"Oh, sure," he snarled. "And while you're at it, why don't you stop off in the kitchen and cook a seven-course meal?" He pointed to a doorway, and I got up and went through the kitchen, which had a stairway leading down to the shop, and into a bedroom with the bathroom next to it. I closed the bedroom door partway behind me, and went to the windows. Sure enough, his bedroom looked right out on the back area, and the back windows of the sperm bank. I went into the bathroom, closed the door, stood around for a second, and flushed the toilet. Then I rejoined Lou and Rosie.

"I've been thinking," he said. "I can't help. He never said anything about going anywhere. He was happy enough at home, although you're right about his folks. They're not much help to him. And if you're thinking he ran away because he did something wrong, don't think it. He wasn't that kind of boy. All he cares about now is his art. Well, mostly all. He cares about his brother. And he likes girls, I guess."

"Any particular girls?"

"I think he has a girlfriend, I forget her name. But you're right. He could have run off with a girl. Kids get funny ideas sometimes."

I hadn't suggested any such thing, but he seemed to like the idea. He liked it so much, I dismissed it as a possibility, for the time being, anyway.

"You must have talked about what he'd do when he grew up, where he'd go to school, where he'd go to work as an artist," Rosie said.

"Well, San Francisco, of course. You can't do better than that."

"Oh, I don't know," Rosie said. "A lot of artists live in

Oakland and Berkeley because they can't afford San Francisco. There's a tremendous amount going on in the East Bay."

He sniffed. An idea too ridiculous, obviously, to contemplate.

"I assume you deal with some San Francisco galleries," I said. "Have you sent any of his work there?"

He shook his head. "I was going to. I've been talking to some people. But no one yet. And no one he knows, if you're thinking that's where he might have gone. Now I wish you'd go. I have an engagement." We allowed him to herd us to the door.

"He's hiding something," Rosie said when we were down on the street again.

I agreed. Lou Overman was hiding, I thought, a whole lot of somethings. But I didn't think he was clever enough to hide them much longer.

— **24** —

We were on our way to the Hackmans when Joanne rolled up behind us.

"Excuse me," she said primly, and we moved out of her way. But before she could go very far, I called out to her.

"Joanne? Did you hear about Rollie Hackman?"

She stopped and spun around halfway to show us her sharp profile. "Yes."

"Do you have any idea where he might have gone or why? Are you friends with him or Tommy?"

"We are not friends." Her mouth twisted in an old-woman smile. "Tommy's stupid and Rollie likes beautiful girls. You know, cheerleaders. That's the dog I saw in your truck, isn't it?"

"Yes," I said.

"Is he friendly?"

"Yes, she is. Any cheerleaders in particular?"

"I wouldn't know. If you'll excuse me, I'm on my way to my great-aunt's house for dinner."

"Oh, is your mother busy tonight?"

She turned away and didn't turn back. "Yes."

She rolled away.

The Hackmans were a mess. Mrs. Hackman was crying and looked as though she didn't plan to stop for days. Hackman was so drunk he couldn't get off the couch. Tommy was holed up in his room and wouldn't come out, but Mrs. Hackman let us go back to see him.

It was just the way Clement had said it was. He wouldn't say anything except "Go away."

Mrs. Hackman, on the other hand, was able and willing, between snuffles, to tell us Rollie's girlfriend's name and address. We got out of the Hackman house as quickly as we could after that. Rosie and I split up at the corner, she to follow up on the girlfriend, I to head back downtown and see if I could find out more about Overman's "engagement" for the evening. We agreed to meet at Georgia's Café in about an hour.

I had nearly reached the gallery when Fredda's station wagon passed me on the street. A couple of seconds later Lou's yellow car pulled out of the alley beside his shop, moving slowly. He turned left onto Main, with Fredda making a U-turn right behind him.

I turned around and ran for the motel and my Chevy. I was going to have to drive fast to catch up with them, and that was going to be hard with one arm. But there wasn't much else I could do. I wanted to see if those two were going to the same place and what they did there.

I started the car and reached over the wheel to shift into first, pulled out of the lot, wrestled the stick into second and then third, drove three blocks, hit a stop sign, ripped off my sling, and used the bad arm to shift. It hurt like hell, but frustration hurts worse.

Catching sight of Fredda's car about a mile outside of town, I followed it from an around-the-curve distance all the way into Rosewood.

She pulled up outside a tavern, parking right behind Lou's car. When she went inside, I parked behind her. I pushed open the door. The place was dimly lit, but I could see the two of them sitting at a booth. I had no hope of not being seen eventually, but I did hope I could at least catch the mood. I did. Lou was talking animatedly, and he looked angry. Fredda was sullen. I couldn't hear what her friend was saying, and tried slithering into a nearby booth. Fredda saw me. Her eyes widened, she muttered something to Lou, then smiled and waved.

I went over to say hello.

"What are you doing here?" Lou snapped.

"Just passing through. Saw your cars, decided to stop in and say hello."

"Hello," he said. "Now would you please leave? This is a private conversation."

"Sure thing. See you two kids around."

I sat in the car for half an hour, put the sling on again, and drove one-handed back to Wheeler, considering the possibilities. Old flames relighting the fire? Hardly. Ma and Pa discussing some problem with the offspring?

Rosie, when we met at Georgia's, had nothing much to report. Rollie's girlfriend said they'd broken up a week before because he wasn't any fun anymore.

"I don't think much of his taste in girls," Rosie said. "She's a real snip, and I don't think she cares about him at all. The only thing she could tell me was that he had some friends down in Marin, she thinks in San Rafael."

"That's something, I guess." I told Rosie what I had been doing.

"Why do you think they'd go out of town to meet?"

"Small town. Gossip. Maybe they don't want Joanne to know they see each other. Maybe they have some other connection, like with Rollie."

At that moment Clement walked into the café. I waved him over and he sat down.

I kept my voice low. "Clement, is Lou Overman Joanne's father?"

"Lou?" He nodded. "But it's not something he or Fredda talk about. No one ever said it was so, even though half the people in town figured it out years ago."

The waitress came. We all ordered chili.

"Why are you asking that, Jake?"

I told him about their meeting in Rosewood. "Did you know they were seeing each other?"

"Seeing each other? How do you mean that?"

"I don't know," I admitted.

"If you're talking about romance, forget it. Those two don't like each other. Not at all. I didn't even know they were speaking. They usually aren't."

"So it's strange that they were together?" Rosie asked.

"Oh, hell, Rosie, maybe they meet each other once a month and talk about old times. It's not the kind of thing I usually look into." He laughed and took a spoonful of chili. I followed his example. It was good.

"Speaking of romance," I said, "what about Hilda and Frank? We saw him bringing her flowers. Now that was strange."

He laughed again. "Oh, Frank has been courting Hilda for years. Wants to get married. Maybe she'll weaken someday. How about you?" He smirked. "I hear you been talking to Melody Clift."

I nodded.

"She tell you anything about her past love life?"

"Of course not."

"Just thought you might be checking into it."

"Why would I do that?" I couldn't tell whether the old bastard was laughing at me or not.

"Well, I thought you might be interested to know she had a fling with Wolf a couple of years ago, before things got so serious with Gracie."

Rosie was enjoying the conversation. "Are you saying she might have been out on the spit the night Gracie died? That she might have killed her in a jealous fit?"

Clement grinned. "Well, she called me early on—you were in the office, Jake—from San Francisco, she said. Lying, maybe, but Henry says he called her later, down there. Still . . ."

"She was on the beach the day the truck got sabotaged," Rosie said.

"That's right, she was on the beach," I said. "Not up on the road with a wrench."

Clement laughed and finished his chili. "Got to go. Checking on a couple of leads about Rollie."

I told him about the friends in San Rafael, but he was ahead of us.

"Yeah. Got some calls in to the police down there, and San Francisco too. Lots of kids run off to San Francisco. Henry's working on it, too, with his newspaper contacts."

I snorted. "He likes to keep his hands on things, doesn't he?"

"Henry's okay. Maybe he cares a little too much, but that's no crime. Guess you didn't much like his piece about you, huh?"

I ignored that. "Before you go, tell me again what exactly it was you found on the beach the day after the break-in?"

"Lot of little plastic vials. Stuck in the sand, caught in the rocks. Had to figure most of them got washed out to sea. We found only a hundred or so. Nora says they lost a lot more than that."

"And that's all you found?"

"You mean footprints, something like that? No, except for Rollie's. Sand was washed smooth of anything that might have been there earlier. Except there was one thing. Big square depression on the dry sand. Could have been made by a box. Could have been what they carried the stuff out there in. But like I said, it was up on the dry sand. Didn't have to even be from that day."

"And Rollie," Rosie said. "He was there."

"That's right. Said he'd been there a little while, hadn't seen anything. See you later." He left.

"Maybe you ought to go talk to Melody again, Jake," Rosie said. "Ask her if she's sure she didn't kill Gracie because Gracie stole her man."

"Enough," I snarled. "Let's follow through on the lovely couple."

"Lou and Fredda?"

"Right. I'll watch his place if you'll watch hers."

"What is it you expect to see?"

"Oh, hell, I don't know. But I would like to know how tight they are, what their relationship is, whether they're sleeping together."

"And if they come back to the same house tonight, one of us will be able to hear what they're talking about?"

"Yes."

The antique store next to Lou's provided good, safe cover. It was a one-story place with no living quarters, all shut up and dark for the night. I brought a blanket from the motel and made a nest for myself behind a dumpster with a good view of Lou's back door. I was wearing two sweaters and a warm jacket. I had no idea how long I'd be stuck there.

As it turned out, I had no more than an hour of discomfort before he drove up the alley, parked behind his shop, and let himself in the back door. Alone. I waited another twenty minutes, just to make sure Fredda wasn't following him, before I set out for Fredda's house. Rosie was waiting for me. She said Fredda had showed up a while ago, with Joanne, and the mother and daughter had gone into the house together. Fredda was asking Joanne, Rosie said, what she had had for dinner at Aunt Hilda's.

—25—

When I woke up the next morning, my arm hurt less and my head felt clearer than it had in days. I left the tape around my shoulder but tossed the gauze sling in the wastebasket.

Waiting for Rosie to get up next door, I reflected that the main problem with this case was the way it attacked from all sides. A burglary, complete with its own handy note of explanation, an explanation that laid what I was sure was a false trail. A murder that looked like an accident, or, possibly, an accident so mired in interconnections that it looked like a murder. An attempted murder, or at least an attempt to scare us off by sabotaging the truck. And now a runaway kid, suspected from the beginning of being the burglar of the first instance.

Put it all together and what happens? What I came up with in that early morning clarity was an amoeba, constantly changing shape, shooting out its little pseudopodia and drawing them in again, but nevertheless an amoeba. One-celled. One case, after all.

Rosie agreed with me, after an argument. Real life, she insisted, wasn't neat. You could very well have a burglary here, an accident there, a crazed attack on a truck still farther over there, and a runaway boy. Maybe, she said, two of them were connected, maybe three, maybe all four. How could you know?

"Wishing," I said, "will make it so."

She chewed on that, along with her paprika-painted country fries.

"What you're saying, then, is that to create order out of chaos we need to pretend there is such a thing as order."

"In all the arts and sciences," I replied, "including the art of detection."

"And do you have a theory that holds this mess together? A framework for your house of cards?"

"There's the unfortunate part," I said. "Several different frameworks can be built."

"Then let's build them. Let's spend the morning seeing if we can't tie up a few loose ends, and then let's stop racing around for a few hours, go sit on the beach, and build them. Maybe when we've put up three or four, one or two will begin to look like they'll stand."

Rosie was looking over my shoulder. "Look who's coming our way."

I turned. It was Henry Linton.

"How are you two doing this morning?" he asked. "How's the arm?"

"Better, thanks," I said politely.

"Good, good . . ."

"Why'd you write that crap in the paper?" I said in the same polite tone of voice.

"Because that's how I feel. Nothing personal. But look what's happened now—young Rollie's disappeared."

"We didn't do it," Rosie said.

"Not saying you did. Like I said, nothing personal. But we don't need people from out of town getting in the way when there's trouble."

"I hear you're going to use some of your contacts to help find Rollie. Contacts out of town," I said.

He smiled. "Can't be helped, now."

"Why don't you want us to find out what's going on?"

He sighed. "I never said that. We need to find out. I just hope you give Clement the credit he deserves when this is all over."

So that was it. He didn't want anyone showing up his sheriff. That really pissed me off. "You know something, Henry? You're a patronizing son of a bitch. Clement's a good lawman. He doesn't need any credit from us. He's doing a great job with no help."

Henry's eyebrows went up. "Except from you."

"We're doing what we can, yeah. But you don't have to take care of Clement. He can take care of himself. So can all the other people you seem to think are your children."

"Well. I guess you told me." He turned and walked out of the restaurant.

We set to work. I called Melody and said I wanted to talk to her, and she invited me for dinner. We checked in with Clement, who had nothing new from San Francisco or San Rafael. He told us he and Perry had finally managed to track down all the summer residents of the spit and the permanent residents who had not been around the week before, and they'd all checked out.

"What about the ones who were around?" Rosie asked. "Are you sure Henry's covered?" He nodded. "What about Frank Wooster?"

"He says he stayed late at the garage Friday, but all we've got is his word. Which reminds me—about Saturday? Henry's got both Frank and Wolf covered for the afternoon. He took his car in to Frank's right after lunch—right after he says he saw you at the restaurant. Then he spent the next three hours working on inventory with Wolf, except for the two or three times he walked over to the garage to check on how Frank was doing. Not much doubt that both Wolf and Frank were working when somebody did in your truck."

Rosie sighed. "Okay. Let's get back to Friday night, then.

What about Marty Spiegel? Have you seen any proof that he was in L.A. until Saturday?"

"He was on the passenger list for an early morning PSA flight and he picked up his ticket, all right."

"What about Hackman?" I interjected. "Has he changed his story on Wolf being at his place?"

"Nope. Of course, if he'd had enough to drink, he might not know if Wolf was there for an hour or fifteen minutes."

That was certainly true. "Thanks, Clement," I said, and started to leave.

"Wait a second, now. I've been thinking . . . You still interested in working with me on some detective stories?"

"You sure you want to do that? It seems like you've got more than enough to do as it is."

"Oh, no. Not most of the time. Things aren't always this busy. And in a couple of years I'll not be working at all." He sounded scared. "I'm going to need to do something." Suddenly, he raised his head and smiled at me. "Otherwise I might wind up getting married."

I laughed, just to show him that I understood he wasn't scared at all. "I think maybe you should do both."

On our way to Frank's garage Rosie attacked. "When are you going to tell that old man the truth?"

"Just as soon as I find someone who would be interested in helping him write those stories."

"Like who?"

"I'm going to talk to Chloe and Artie at *Probe*, see what they come up with."

"And what if Clement really has nothing to say, or can't say it even with help, or what if no one wants to bother to find out whether he can or not?"

"I don't know. But if someone who really knows talks to him, it might work out okay. Meanwhile, I think we ought to encourage him to make a pass at his office help."

"Angie?"

"I don't mean Perry. Yeah, he likes her."

"I never noticed."

"That's the trouble with women. No romance. No sensitivity."

Frank was sitting in his chair again, but a skinny man with red hair was working on the truck.

"Body man," he grunted. "Maybe found a fender too. Not sure yet."

"Great," Rosie said.

"Read the piece about you in the *Weekly*. Going to take the hint?" We didn't say anything. "Don't like you pestering Hilda. You got no right to bother decent people."

"We'll remember that," Rosie said. "When will the truck be finished?"

"Soon, I hope."

"Clement says you were here when Gracie died," I said. "Is that true?"

He got out of his chair and joined the body man inside the garage.

I decided against hitting him over the head and dragging him back out into the daylight. Instead, we walked away, down to the main cross street, Cellini Avenue, that led to the beach. And kept walking, both silent, thinking, along the sand. We had passed the Spicer Street access and were on our way to the spit before Rosie spoke.

"Why are we walking so far?"

"Subconscious. Our minds are telling us Gracie's death is the key to the whole thing."

"Don't start going mystical on me." She took off her shoes and socks. "Besides, I think the burglary is the key."

She sat down on the damp sand and began scooping it into a pile in front of her. I took off my shoes and socks, too, rolled up my pants, and sat down beside her. The sun was almost warm, the sand was cold. I helped her scoop sand. Alice, who had chased enough sea gulls, went to sleep.

"Let's start with both," I said. "Gracie and the bank. Let's start with Gracie going through the donor profiles but not following up."

"And she has a fiancé, or at least a boyfriend. Say he's become sterile. She wants a kid anyway. The idea enrages him, or at least insults him."

"So he trashes the place, does a symbolic dumping of his rivals. But she says she's going to do it anyway. He can't stand the thought. He kills her. He sets up an alibi with a drunken friend."

Rosie held up a sand-caked hand. "That leaves out Rollie."

"He was on the beach that morning. He saw something. After he saw what happened to Gracie and to us, he got scared and took off."

She had collected a big pile of sand by now, and was shaping it into a two-by-two-by-one-foot-tall block. "Except for one thing." She was smoothing the top of her block, evening it out. Then she began scooping sand up and piling it into a second level. "It doesn't explain why Wolf, as the vandal, would go through the donor files."

"Why would anyone?"

"Curiosity," she said doubtfully. "Or whoever did it was looking for something specific. I lean toward that second alternative."

She had found an ice cream stick and was cutting crenellations along the lower wall of her castle. She must have gotten bored, because she dropped the stick and returned to shaping the second-level tower. I picked up the stick and continued, for a while, the tedious and repetitive work she had begun on the lower wall.

"We need to find out why Gracie was looking for a donor," I said. "I wonder, do you think Lou and Wolf are friends?"

She was having trouble with the tower. The sand kept crumbling away. I cut a doorway in the lower wall. "You mean Lou wouldn't tell on a friend if he saw him breaking into the sperm bank?"

"Right." I was smoothing a road from the castle to some-where else. "They broke in here. Then they packed the stuff into a box and carried it off to there." I ran my hand down the beach a way, and then toward the water.

"But why didn't they just carry it down to here?" Rosie cut a direct route from the castle to the water. "Why not take it down Cellini to the first, closest beach?"

"Because they thought they'd be more likely to be seen closer to downtown?"

"I guess." She didn't look convinced.

"I wonder where Frank Wooster was when Gracie died, and why he doesn't want us talking to Hilda."

"I wonder," Rosie said, "what Rollie knows." She got the tower to stay in one piece. I finished the crenellations, al-though the last dozen or so got pretty sloppy. We sat back and looked at it. "Do we still have that map Clement drew?" she asked. "With the streets and the beaches on it?"

I nodded. "Yeah. Somewhere." I could see where she was going—where we were both going. We began to plan our next moves.

—26—

Rosie wanted to talk to the Hackmans again. I volunteered for another Fredda detail.

We walked back along the beach as far as Spicer, up Spicer into the town, and separated with a promise to meet at the tavern.

Fredda was sitting on the ramp, in the sun, with her eyes closed. She didn't know I was there until I said hello. She jumped, and glared at me.

"Scared me half to death," she muttered.

I apologized and told her I wanted to talk about Gracie again.

"Well, Jesus," she whined, "I can't imagine why."

"If you're working, I'd be happy to sit in the kitchen with you."

"No. I'm taking a break. Fire away." I sat down beside her.

"I keep thinking about Gracie going through those donor profiles over at the bank."

"Why?"

"Because there must have been a reason. Something wrong between her and Wolf maybe? Something wrong with him? She must have said something, sometime."

"Well . . ." She was being coy, and it wasn't attractive.

"I'm sure you want to know what really happened to your cousin."

She shrugged. "I think she fell, but okay, there is something I can tell you, just to get you off my back for a while." Suddenly, she did something really ghastly. She slid her rear end over a few inches and rubbed her shoulder against mine. She laughed. "Off my back. Pretty funny, right?"

I did my best to ignore her heavy-handed overture, while at the same time continuing to appear friendly, even concerned. "Wonderful." I smiled. "I knew you'd want to help."

"Where's your girlfriend?"

That stopped me for a second, until I realized she meant Rosie.

"My friend"—I underscored the word—"is busy elsewhere." I try to make a habit of laying no claim to Rosie as anything but a friend, partly, maybe, so I can keep our relationship clear to myself. This was one of those times, though, when I probably should have kept my mouth shut.

"That's nice. Now, you want to know about Gracie and Wolf. It's true. They were having arguments. Not in public or anything, but she did say they were having problems. She didn't say what kind and I didn't ask. Just problems, and she wasn't real happy, and I don't think she knew what she was going to do. Is that what you wanted to hear?"

"Only if it's so." She performed another ghastly act by favoring me with her giggle.

"About children," I said. "Was she particularly eager to have a child? She was in her thirties, and I know some women get strong feelings around then about children."

"Oh, yes. She always said she wanted children."

"Now, once again, something I've asked you about before. Wolf has had a child, so, as far as we know, he doesn't have any sterility problems, or didn't have—"

"Do you?"

"What?"

"I'll bet you don't."

Oh, Christ, I thought. "He's had a child—" I caught myself. I'd already said that. "If he's okay, and they were still considering marriage, why was she looking through those files?"

"Well, it's obvious, isn't it?" Fredda said. "She must have decided she wasn't going to marry him at all."

"So you think she might decide, then, to go ahead and have a child more or less on her own?"

"Why not? Lots of people do that. Lots of people have children even though they're not married. Sometimes it's by accident, but sometimes it's on purpose."

I told her I understood all that.

She stood up. Her mood had changed again. "I need to go back to work. Is that all you need?"

It wasn't. Far from it. But there was just so much of this woman I could take, especially without Rosie there as a buffer. I let Fredda go back to her cookies.

Despite the depression Fredda had washed over me, my spirits rose as I walked back through town. Maybe it was true that Gracie and Wolf were having problems. That Gracie wanted to have a child by means of the sperm bank. So what if she hadn't followed up on it? She hadn't really had the time, had she?

Wolf wasn't looking so good. He was sitting on a stool

behind the bar, slumped over with misery and weariness. No one else was there.

"How you doing?" I asked cheerily.

"Okay. What'll you have?"

"Draft."

He filled a glass, placed it carefully on the bar in front of me. Before I had a chance to say anything more to him, he walked to the other end of the bar.

Rosie walked in. She said hello politely to Wolf, he said hello politely to her. She ordered a beer and we took them over to a table far enough away so we could whisper without being overheard by the man behind the bar.

Hackman had been home alone, she said, and he'd been reasonably sober. Depressed about Rollie, but sober.

"Maybe his kid running away will get to him, make him change," I said.

"I doubt it, but maybe. Anyway, he insists that Wolf spent his entire dinner hour with him. That he was at his house from a couple of minutes after five to just before six. He says he remembers it clearly."

"Hmmph," I said.

"I talked to him about Overman, too, and his relationship with the boy. He says Rollie worshipped the man. Would do anything for him."

"What else?"

"Henry. I ran into him on the street. He absolutely, positively, and definitely denied that Wolf and Gracie were anything but perfectly happy and planning their marriage. He says it was wonderful, how happy Wolf was." I told her what Fredda had said. She shook her head. "Not according to Henry. He also says it's a damned shame you and I don't leave 'the boy' alone. That's what he called him. Loves him like a son, he said."

"Christ." I told her about the rest of my visit with Fredda. "That woman wears me down," I said. "I'm taking the night off. Got a date with Melody."

"I've got a date too."

"With who, Nora?" I sincerely hoped not.

She laughed. "Hardly. It's Dr. Reid."

"The medical consultant at the bank?" She nodded. "Well, how about that."

"Since you're seeing Melody tonight, why don't you ask her if she killed Gracie in a fit of jealousy—you know, just to get her out of the way as a suspect."

"Shut up. There are a couple of things I want to ask Wolf, though. Want another beer?"

"Sure."

I ambled up to the bar. "Two more, Wolf." He began to draw the beer. "Mind if I ask you something?"

He turned off the tap. "Yes."

"Great. Seems Gracie was checking out the donor profiles over at the sperm bank a couple of weeks ago. Any idea why she might have done that?"

He stared at me. "I don't know. She worked there."

"It didn't have anything to do with work as far as we can tell. Was she really going to marry you?"

His face was getting red. "Yes." Were those tears in his eyes?

"Then maybe there's some problem? With you, I mean?"

His face was nearly purple. He slammed a half-filled stein down on the bar, splashing beer on both of us. "I'm going to rip your balls off." He vaulted over the bar, right into me, knocking me to the floor. I scrambled to my feet. Rosie was suddenly beside me. I saw the punch coming barely in time to jerk my head aside. He missed my face but sideswiped my neck, and the blow was hard enough just glancing by to make me see a few flashing lights. While I was watching the fireworks, he was getting his hands around my neck, trying to force me back and down, choking me.

Rosie picked up a barstool and brought it down on his back. He yelled and fell off me. Then he collapsed in a heap on the floor, sobbing.

Rosie went to him, put her hand on his shoulder. He didn't push her away. He looked up at her, his eyes streaming tears. I thought maybe he was going to gaze into her big brown ones and confess everything. Instead, between sobs, he asked her, "What's he talking about?" Then an amazing thing happened. Rosie sat down on the floor beside him and cradled his head against her shoulder.

That was when Henry walked in. He stood in the doorway and gaped at us. Rosie and Wolf on the floor making nice, and me, leaning against the bar, holding my neck.

He walked over to where Wolf sat, his head still against Rosie's shoulder, and helped him to his feet.

"I don't know what's been going on here," he said, "but I think this boy needs a doctor."

Wolf shook his head. "No. I'm okay now. I just can't take any more of this guy's shit, that's all. He won't let me get my mourning done." The last few words came out in an eerie wail. He shook his head again, and wandered off toward the men's room. "Just need to wash my face." Before he went through the door, though, he stopped, turned around, and looked at Rosie, a soft, grateful, almost apologetic look.

She muttered something that sounded like "Sure. Okay." Henry said he thought it would be best if we'd leave. I agreed with him.

"That was very touching," I said to Rosie.

"Oh, for God's sake," she snapped, "what's the matter with you, anyway, premenstrual syndrome? Haven't you ever lost someone you loved?" The question was rhetorical. She knew very well that I had. More than once.

I was beginning to worry about Rosie. Was she attracted to the man? I was having enough trouble thinking objectively as it was. I wanted her to be able to.

"While you're feeling so damned sorry for him, are you forgetting the possibility that he killed her? Just because he's feeling bad now doesn't mean he didn't do it."

We walked half a block in silence. "And just because you don't like him," she said, "and you don't like the alternatives, doesn't mean he did. The things that are starting to add up aren't adding up to Wolf. And you know it." I knew it, all right, and neither one of us liked the alternatives.

I was due at Melody's for dinner, but I left the motel earlier than I needed to, and made a point of pulling up outside Frank Wooster's place to take another look at it. He didn't seem to be home. I got out of the car and stood near his front door, facing the ocean, facing the point where Gracie had fallen, right across from Spiegel's house. If Gracie had been standing out there right that minute, I would have had a clear view of her. I noticed that Wooster had not yet taken the boards off his front windows, although the weather had been fair for days. Maybe he didn't like the view.

There was a light on at Filomena's. I made a quick decision to stop by.

She was happy to see me, and offered me a glass of brandy. I said no thanks, I was on my way somewhere else and had just wanted to say hello. And I wanted to ask her again what she might have seen the night of Gracie's death.

"I know you didn't see her, didn't see anything of what happened to her. But maybe you saw something else? Something small, something you might not have considered significant."

"But what could that be?"

"Did you see any of your neighbors? Talk to them? See anyone arriving before you closed up your house?"

She thought about it. "No. Nothing. Mr. Spiegel's house was dark, of course, and the people next door were away too." The cat, Sara, appeared in the doorway, brushed briefly against my leg, and darted off into the yard. "Frank was home a bit earlier than usual. His garage doesn't usually close until five, and then he tends to eat dinner in town, I think. But he was out there, boarding up his windows. Other than that, I didn't hear or see anything."

"Frank? Frank Wooster was home? Here? Next door? What time was that?"

"It must have been sometime around four, or closer to four-thirty, actually. I saw him hammering up some plywood right before I closed my shutters. He was just getting started, too, poor man."

She didn't think he'd seen her, she said. I didn't think he had, either.

I wanted to kiss her on the cheek, but I didn't. I thanked her and went on to Melody's. Melody was curious about the private call I wanted to make, but left me alone with her gilded French reproduction phone. Clement was home. He said he'd go have a talk with Frank.

"I should have checked back with the Barth woman," he said. "Perry's the one who talked to her. I should have known better."

"Don't be too hard on Perry," I said. "I talked to her once before too."

—27—

Dinner at Melody's was a great success, from the marinated artichoke hearts to the mousse. I was astonished and nearly overcome with admiration when she carried in the stuffed trout.

"You made this?"

"Of course not," she admitted. "My cook did."

"Is she still in the kitchen? I want to tell her—"

"Him. And he's gone for the night, of course. Why would I want him to stay?"

Anyway, like I said, it was a great success all the way

around. For one thing, I had never before made love in a hexagonal tower.

The stairway to the bedroom rose from a corner of the large living room. I guess you could call it winding, but it wasn't like those dizzy, tight little spirals that take up maybe five or six feet of space in a room. It was big enough to get you through the ceiling in two wide turns. It was heavily carpeted, enclosed with a waist-high rail, and it didn't quiver.

Melody led the way. At that point, I probably could have followed her up a twenty foot ladder without hesitating.

I came up through the ceiling and stepped onto a slate floor partly covered by several overlapping Persian rugs, all of them red. To my right, its head against one side of the hexagon, was a round brass bed. I didn't know there was such a thing, and there probably isn't—unless you can have one handmade. The head and foot formed arc-shapes that partially enclosed the red-velvet-covered mattress and made me think of a crib in a whorehouse.

Three walls of the hexagon were window. The other three, including the one the bed rested against, were paneled with something exotic—cypress?—and pale and hung with erotic tapestries, heavy and old-looking. Greek stuff. Satyrs and maids and shepherds and nymphs. I'd heard about satyrs before, but I'd had no idea of the extent of their, well, extent.

Feeling momentarily mortal, I walked over to the window walls. The glass was warm, double glass, heated by vents between the two layers. I looked out over the shrubbery, over the road, to the cliff and the ocean beyond it. The sky was clear, the Pacific washed noisily and rhythmically against the rocks. My focus shifted and I saw Melody lying propped against the pillows on the bed, smiling, watching me. I forgot about the satyr and concentrated on the nymphs.

I woke early and alone. Thin fog was drifting against the windows. The smell of coffee drifted up from downstairs. I dressed and went down to the living room. Melody was there, and someone else was working in the kitchen. She kissed me on the cheek and went to tell the cook to put breakfast on.

The man—he looked like a bodybuilder—served us and then left the house. I don't know where he came from or where he went. He smiled, but he never said a word. I wondered if she carted him around with her wherever she traveled.

I sat down to a beautiful breakfast across from a beautiful, if somewhat tired-looking, woman, and that was when I learned that, unfortunately, my first time in the tower was also my last, and that this breakfast was a good-bye meal.

"You're going back to San Francisco?" I asked, swallowing a mouthful of shirred eggs. I had not yet gotten the point of what she was saying.

"Not yet, Jake. I'm sorry. I hope you won't be upset. But Wolf needs me."

I didn't remind her that she had called him a "dumb hunk." He'd gotten to her somehow. He sure had a way with women.

She said she felt torn, but believed she was doing the right thing "for now." She said she had wanted us to have "one last beautiful night together" before she told me she was going to start seeing Wolf again.

"I understand," I said, always a good sport. I didn't, but then no one ever said I had to.

Rosie answered my knock on her motel room door dressed and ready for breakfast. On the way to Georgia's, I told her about Frank Wooster. We stopped in at the police station, but Clement wasn't in yet. I asked Angie to tell him where we would be for the next hour. She wrote the message down very carefully.

We had a big day ahead of us, but I still couldn't bring myself to eat breakfast twice. I ordered coffee, Rosie ordered half the menu.

"Didn't the doctor give you breakfast?"

"Not everyone works as fast as you do, my friend."

I laughed, "Fast doesn't always take." I told her about Melody and Wolf. She patted my hand and looked carefully at me.

"How do you feel?"

"My ego's a little bruised, I guess. And my feelings. But I'm okay—I mean, Lee's the one I really—"

She shook her head at me, grinning. "Lee would love to know that. How's your neck feel?"

"That's bruised, too." I pulled down my sweater's turtleneck and showed her. "But not bad."

She sipped her coffee. "Had any more thoughts about sandcastles?"

"And maps," I said, pulling out of my pocket the map Clement had drawn for us, smoothing it out on the table between us.

"And famous men?"

I nodded, and drew a couple more items on the map. Like kids playing Connect the Dots, we sketched some lines from point to point. What we came up with wasn't the bunny in the tree, but it was just as good.

Clement came in and sat down with us for a cup of coffee. He'd talked to Wooster, he said, and the old man had admitted he'd been home but insisted he had seen nothing.

"Sure," I said. "That's why he lied about being there in the first place."

"I'll keep on his back," Clement said, finishing his coffee and taking off again.

Rosie said there was some research she wanted to do in Rosewood. I told her to take the Chevy, I thought I could handle my end of things without a car.

"Isn't it interesting," she mused, "what kinds of ideas you can come up with if you take a situation and skew it just a little? Take an action and look at it from another side?"

"You think we're on it now, don't you?"

"Yes. It makes sense, in a crazed kind of way."

We agreed that sometimes it pays to spend a few hours building sand castles. But we had a few more moves to make, a few more right answers to get before we could justify what we were planning for later that night.

Rosie went off to do her research. I went to visit Aunt Hilda one more time, then I stopped in at Wooster's garage. He told me the truck would be as ready as he could make it in a day or two.

"Terrific," I said. "How come you lied about being out on the spit when Gracie died?"

He did exactly what I'd expected him to do. He turned around and started walking away.

"I'll get back to you on that tomorrow," I said.

Marty Spiegel's car wasn't anywhere on Main Street, so I called him and asked him to meet me at the motel. He said he had to stick around and keep an eye on the roofers, but he'd drive in and pick me up if I wanted him to.

I did. I hadn't gotten nearly enough sleep the night before and a walk out to the spit and back was more than I wanted to do.

Spiegel and I spent a pleasant couple of hours together. The roofers were there hammering away, but the day was sunny and warm and we sat out on the patio drinking tequila sunrises and talking about the town and the people in it, talking about death and reproduction. I confessed that I had read his file and knew about the arrangement he'd made for his sperm. I asked him how much Gracie knew about that arrangement.

All she knew, he said, was that he was a donor.

Had she ever asked him about it? No, he said, she hadn't. Not directly.

"She did start to talk about it once, the last time I was up here, but I got kind of embarrassed and changed the subject. I don't like to talk about it much. Like it's bad luck or something."

"When was that—the time she started to talk about it?"

"Couple of months ago, I think. Can we get off it now?"

I got off it, but not very far. I asked him about other women in town. If he'd been interested in anyone or if anyone had shown an interest in him. Then we talked about his neighbors on the spit, particularly Frank Wooster. And we talked about Overman and Joanne.

I didn't tell him where I was going with any of this conversation, but he's a smart man. He got the idea. And the minute he got it, he changed the subject. He told me a bit more about how he'd made his fortune, and I told him more about how much fun it was to be a detective. He asked if I'd be interested in being a consultant for one of his films someday, and mentioned a very tempting figure.

He offered to drive me back to town, but I felt like walking off the tequila and the conversation. After talking to him, I didn't have much doubt, anymore, about what had happened to Gracie Piedmont and why. I took the path down to the beach and strolled along the water until I came to the spot where the vials had been dumped. Then I cut up and across the road and into town, up Spicer to Mendocino.

I saw Hackman working under the hood of the junk car in his driveway and said hello. I saw Joanne rolling down the street toward her house and waved to her. She waved back, hunched her narrow shoulders, and wheeled up the ramp to her front porch.

One quick stop at the hardware store, and then on to the motel.

Rosie was there already. We exchanged the day's information. We called Clement to see if there was anything new on Frank or on Rollie. There wasn't. I told him what Spiegel had said and what Rosie had learned that day. He said we were getting closer but he couldn't move on it yet. I didn't tell him what we were planning for later that night. I couldn't.

Meanwhile, the best thing Rosie and I could do for the next few hours was sleep. It would be the last chance we'd have for a while.

As I was dozing off, I thought about Melody. I was glad she had, at least, felt torn—whatever the hell that meant.

— *28*—

About one in the morning we crept around the back of the sperm bank. I had a piece of glass I'd bought at the hardware store, a few inches square. Rosie had a cardboard carton she'd filled with cheap plastic toys from the dime store.

I stood up against the building, just below the window that had been entered the night of the burglary, and dropped my piece of glass to the asphalt of the parking lot. It broke. Rosie scraped her carton along the side of the building and set it down on the ground. The contents made small noises of collision. I grabbed the box and we both dashed around the side of the bank, just as we heard a window being raised. I lay down on the ground and peeked out from behind a garbage can. Overman had his head stuck out his bedroom window and was looking all around the back area for the source of the sounds. Then he pulled his head back in and slammed the window.

So much for Lou the sound sleeper. It didn't prove anything, but it fit in with the picture we were developing very well, especially the part about Rollie Hackman.

We headed for Mendocino Street.

A darker night would have been better. The half moon was bright. The streets were empty of life. Not so much as a cat in a yard. Just us, standing out like clowns at a wake.

We made our way up the driveway to the back door of Fredda's house, up the ramp to the porch. The key was where I hoped it would be, under the flowerpot where we'd seen Joanne replace it the first day we'd visited the house.

I put the key in the lock and turned it, very slowly, very carefully. It made a scraping noise that sounded, to us, like an alarm clock. We ducked down and waited. No lights went on. No voices. I turned the knob and pushed the door open. A hinge squeaked. A drop of cold sweat trickled down my cheek.

I was hating every second of it. I hate the sick-stomach feeling I get when I'm breaking into someone else's house or falling downstairs or getting caught by someone's spouse or lover. It's times like this when I wonder why I do this kind of work. I don't like that feeling of dread that I'm sure is like a drug to people who walk between skyscrapers on tight wires. I didn't want to get caught. We had no right to be there. We had a lot of pieces that fit, that was all. No real proof. And this was not exactly a legal way to catch a criminal. But then, I told myself, I'm not a legal detective and Rosie's a carpenter, so what the hell did we care?

We tiptoed across the kitchen floor to the freezer and opened it. The light from inside glared like a thousand kliegs. We began to search, methodically removing plastic bags of cookies from the shelves and replacing them exactly where they had been before.

Rosie found it. A small plastic bag. Inside, two small plastic tubes, no bigger than my thumb. Each one had the number 126 taped to it. Marty Spiegel's donor number.

— 29 —

Having finished our sneaking around for the night, we went back to the motel to get Alice before we made our next stop.

Clement wasn't happy to see us at three in the morning.

"What's happened?" he wanted to know. "What have you found out?"

"We're sure now," Rosie said. "If you get a search warrant, you'll find the evidence at Fredda's."

"What evidence? And what makes you sure?"

This was the tricky part. "She stole the sperm," I said. "And she kept some of it. We're sure because we've been up all night putting it together."

He squinted at me. "I've already heard your theory. I asked you why you're sure now."

"Pure deduction," I said righteously. "We just put more of the pieces together, and—bingo!"

He looked at me. He looked at Rosie. Our bright, innocent, eager faces showed nothing but joy. He grinned sourly.

"Let's have some coffee," he said. "Then you can tell me all about it. Or maybe I should say almost all about it."

"First of all," I began when we were all settled around the coffee table with our cups, "there were so many little things that didn't quite make sense, or that made sense only one way. Starting with the burglary, why did the thief take the stuff halfway to the spit before dumping it? To the beach past Spicer? The access at Cellini is much closer to the bank. And Lou—did you ever really believe he heard nothing that night?"

"It's possible."

I told him about our experiment earlier that evening. "Again, it doesn't mean much all by itself, but it fits. It fits if he was involved or was trying to protect someone. Then there's the burglary itself. There never was any way to tell if some of the vials were missing. And if the burglars were out for pure destruction, why did they just go through the files and mess them up?"

"Take it back a couple of months," Rosie said. "Gracie worked at the bank. She was a friend of Spiegel's. She knew he was a donor of some kind. She also must have known it was a very private thing to him. Yet she tried to get him to talk about it. He wouldn't, but she gave it a try. Then a couple of weeks ago she used her job at the bank to go through the donor profiles—the public information. Why? She's supposed to be marrying Wolf, and as far as we can tell, he's okay—enough to have fathered a child a few years ago, anyway."

"And a week after that the confidential files are rifled and the sperm stolen," I said.

"And Fredda's attitude toward Spiegel was a little strange," Rosie added. "She seemed jealous somehow, and she said he was a snob. He doesn't seem to be. What did he do that would make her say that? And that brings us to Gracie's death. She was with Fredda that afternoon. Spiegel called. Now Spiegel says he just asked Gracie if she knew whether things were okay on the spit and she volunteered to go out and look. Fredda says he asked her to go out there. Let's say Spiegel's telling the truth. She volunteered. Why? Because she was crazy about him? Or because she wasn't having such a great time with Fredda and wanted to leave?"

"And think back," I said, "to that night out on the spit. When Fredda got out of her car she had mud all the way up her boots. The deep mud was out on the edge, where Gracie went over—and Fredda hadn't gone out there when any of us were around. Sure, she could have picked up the mud somewhere else, but again, it fit. I got muddy that night. Rosie just got wet. And of course there was one big question—why did Gracie go out on the edge at all? She didn't. Not by herself, anyway. Now add the peculiar behavior of two more people: Frank Wooster, who lied about being home that afternoon, and Rollie Hackman, who's disappeared. Where does that take you?"

"You tell me, city boy," Clement said, smiling.

"It takes you right to Fredda, all the way down the line. Fredda, who thought it was so wonderful that Nora's folks had it made for life because Nora was bright and successful. Fredda, who had a daughter who was not only disabled, but didn't seem to be much interested in anything but Hilda's brand of religion, and certainly didn't seem to be wild about her mother.

"Yesterday, when I talked to Spiegel, I asked him if Fredda had ever made a pass at him. She had, a couple of months ago. She told him she wanted him to father her child. He turned her down. It wasn't long after that that Fredda's cousin, Gracie, asked him about his donor status at the bank. Everyone we talked to about Gracie gave us a picture of a docile, sweet, dependent kind of woman. Nora said she was a follower. Fredda's crazy as hell, but she's strong and dominant and she goes after what she wants.

"Fredda's next step was obvious. With Gracie's help she would find out if becoming a client at the bank would get her the child of a rich and famous man."

"And that didn't work either, because his genes weren't for sale," Rosie said. "So she stole them. And she laid a false trail by leaving that 'religious' note and by stealing all the vials and making it look like all of them were dumped in the ocean. I don't know whether her pointing the finger at religion was malicious, because she hated Hilda, or just the easiest way—the first thing she thought of. Anyway, she packed the stuff up, drove home—she must have had some idea about how perishable it is—stuck what she wanted into the freezer, and took the rest of it down Spicer to the nearest beach."

"And Gracie," Clement said, "wouldn't have a lot of doubt about who the burglar was."

"And being a good employee, and probably a decent enough person," I said, "she was more than a little upset that she had, in a way, been a party to the crime. She was distracted, she was worried—and she must have let Fredda know how she felt. I suspect they were arguing about it when Spiegel called that night. Fredda'd gone through a lot by then. She'd worked hard. She wasn't about to let Gracie ruin it. When Gracie volunteered to go to Spiegel's—as much to get away from her cousin as anything else, I'll bet—Fredda followed her. I'd guess she whacked her over the head, dragged her out to the edge, and tossed her over.

"Then she went back to Gracie's, waited awhile, and called the cops."

"There was another crime too," Clement reminded me unnecessarily.

I poured myself another cup of coffee. My arm still ached a bit. "Fredda was one of several people who could have known where we were going that morning. You and Angie knew. Henry could have overheard us in the restaurant. Mrs. Hackman must have heard us too, even though she says she doesn't remember catching any of our conversation. And Fredda came in to deliver some cookies and spent some time talking to Mrs. Hackman."

"Or," Rosie said, "by chance she could have spotted the truck parked there. I checked with that new client of hers up in Rosewood, the Italian restaurant, a few miles up the coast road. Fredda delivered some cookies there that morning. They didn't know what time exactly, but it wasn't long after we crashed."

"Any number of people could have killed Gracie," I concluded. "Wolf had a lousy alibi. But Fredda? It was only her word that she sat around and waited for Gracie to come back."

"You're leaving out a couple of important folks," Clement argued. "Three, as a matter of fact: Lou, Rollie, Frank."

"Especially Frank," Rosie agreed.

"Lou too," I said. "And that angry little discussion he was having with Fredda the night I followed them. And the fact that he acts like he knows something about Rollie he's not telling."

30

Clement went off to get his warrant; Rosie and I went to visit Lou Overman. We still didn't know what part he'd played, but the last thing we needed was another inconvenient disappearance.

"We know what happened," I told him. "Rollie's gone through enough. Tell the truth."

He let us in, but he wasn't ready for truth yet. "What do you mean, you know what happened?"

"We know what Fredda did."

"You can't prove it," he quavered. I wanted to break his nose.

"We can," Rosie said.

"I'll hear it from Clement."

"Fine," I said. "He knows where we are. We'll just sit quiet and wait for him."

It was a long couple of hours. Lou made breakfast—for himself only—choked some of it down, and ran to the bathroom to throw it up. I couldn't remember when I'd had a better time on an empty stomach.

When Clement finally showed up, he said Frank Wooster, faced with the fact of Fredda's arrest, had talked, and he'd fill us in later, "when we were finished with Lou." He glared at Lou when he said it.

"Henry's newspaper friends are going to run some pieces telling Rollie he can come home now, because we know everything," Clement said to Lou. "This is your big chance to be a hero, Overman."

The slimy little bastard broke down.

What happened was this: The night of the burglary at the sperm bank he heard a noise and looked out his window to see Fredda loading her wagon. She saw him watching her.

"We just stared at each other," he said. "I saw the broken window. I didn't know what was going on, but Fredda's never been anything but trouble to me—" He stopped, looking almost guilty. "Anyway, I just backed up and went to bed again. But would she leave me out of it? Oh, no."

She called him. She said if he told, she'd say he was in on it, that he'd helped her. She told him what she had done and why, and that it was his "duty" to keep quiet. And she told him she'd left something on the beach that belonged to him.

"She was always trying to torture me," he whined. "I thought she was probably lying, but I couldn't take a chance." He drove out to the beach. Up on the sand above the water line he found the carton she'd carried the vials in— a book carton from a publishing company.

"She's always using them for her cookies," he said. "It wouldn't have implicated me any more than her. It was just her idea of a joke, to scare me, to get me out there. To compromise me. But I took it. I picked it up. And that was when Rollie came along with his sketch pad."

"And he couldn't tell the law he'd seen his idol—his patron—out there that morning," Rosie said.

"We never talked about it. Never. I never told him not to tell."

"That helped a lot," I said.

"And did you know she killed Gracie?" Rosie asked him.

"How could I know that?"

"Weren't you afraid she'd kill you too?"

"I wouldn't tell. She knew I wouldn't."

Through that whole long conversation he never once admitted why Fredda thought it was his "duty" not to tell. Never admitted that Joanne was his child.

Frank Wooster, on the other hand, wasn't at all shy about admitting why he'd lied about the night of the murder. He had seen Gracie drive by. A few minutes later, when he was just finishing up with the windows at the side of his house, he saw Fredda following.

A few minutes after that, he said, he "heard a yell." But he "didn't think nothing about it" until later, when he heard what had happened.

The fact was, he said, he'd never really lied, except about being at the garage, because he didn't know that Fredda had done anything wrong, and "I never said I didn't see Fredda out there, and I never saw her hurt her cousin."

He hadn't wanted to get Fredda into trouble, he said, because then Hilda would have to take Joanne, and he and Joanne didn't get along. An item Hilda had confirmed the last time I'd talked to her.

I couldn't help but wonder if there was something more to it. Maybe he actually approved of what Fredda had done. But even Frank Wooster didn't have nerve enough to say that.

Henry did what he said he was going to do, and Rollie spotted the story in a Marin County newspaper. He came home.

The boy, who had suffered so much trying to protect his hero, who had run away so no one could "make" him tell, managed to turn things around so that Lou came out looking noble for trying to protect his family. Even if Lou didn't admit to having one.

When Rosie and I collected our pay from Nora, she told us the bank had some catching up to do, and some lawsuits to deal with, but it would win and it would survive. I never doubted it would.

As for Fredda, well, there are some people who just can't win. Aside from being charged with murder and assorted other crimes, she'd done it all for nothing.

Gracie had apparently given her sketchy information about the insemination process. She knew the sperm had to be kept frozen, and that it would die quickly if it thawed. And it had thawed by the time she got it home. So, just to be sure, she stuck the three vials in the home freezer. Instant spermicide.

The next day she thawed one vial of dead sperm and used it. And sat back and waited for the pregnancy that was going to safeguard her old age.

About her role in the truck crash—that was the one thing no one could pin on her for sure. All we had was her probable presence on the road that day, and the information I'd gotten from Hilda when I'd persuaded her to elaborate on some of the things Fredda, in her poverty, had learned to do for herself. Among them, Hilda had told me, was minor maintenance and repair on her station wagon.

Clement asked Fredda if she'd written the "religious" note that had been left at the bank with her left hand and she just laughed at him.

The good police chief had mixed feelings about the whole thing. His colleagues in law enforcement thought he'd done some pretty hot police work, and that was good. But he said the case had left a bad taste in his mouth, and writing detective stories looked better all the time. He gave me a manila envelope stuffed with neatly typed sheets of paper.

"Angie helped me," he said with a smile. "She typed it all up."

I agreed to read it over and talk to "some people." The truth was, I never intended to read it myself. My friends at *Probe* were a lot better equipped than I was to do that. If it was any good at all, I figured I could slide out of the picture by turning him over to someone who could really help him.

If it wasn't any good? I'd worry about that when I came to it. Maybe Angie would help me worry about it.

It was no surprise to anyone, least of all to Frank Wooster, when Joanne moved in with Great-aunt Hilda. We didn't know whether either of them had known or even suspected what Fredda was doing, and Clement said he didn't want to know. I wouldn't have been surprised to find out that Joanne had it all worked out from the beginning.

The day we left town, Rosie and I saw the girl wheeling

down Main Street and stopped to talk. I was hoping she wouldn't hate us for what had happened to Fredda.

"How are you doing, Joanne?" Rosie asked.

"Fine. Are you sure your dog doesn't bite?"

"Positive. Go ahead, pet her." The child touched the dog briefly, nervously, on the top of the head, but pulled her hand away when Alice tried to lick it.

"I'm sorry about your mother," I said.

"We both are," Rosie told her.

Joanne looked at us suspiciously, saw that we meant it, and laughed. A bitter little snicker.

"I'm not," she said. "You think I don't know she never liked me? And I never liked her. I'm glad. Now I get to live with Aunt Hilda. Where I belong."

Joanne rolled away and we watched her go. I felt a little sick, and Rosie didn't look too happy, either. I knew we'd talk about it later, at home, but neither one of us felt much like talking right then.

I got into my Chevy. Rollie Hackman's watercolor of the triangle rocks lay on the back seat, carefully wrapped. For just a second, I thought about detouring out to the spit to say good-bye to Melody, but the thought passed.

Rosie aimed her truck south and I pulled out into the road behind her. We headed back to the Bay Area, where we belong.